Born in Australia, John Stanley Dennis grew up working on sheep and cattle stations, then knocked around at all kinds of work, got caught up in the hippy generation, built a 30 ft yacht, lived on it in the Daintree River for a time, then moved on working at a safari camp and building a home. He now lives in South Burnett in Queensland, Australia

JOHN STANLEY DENNIS

Are You John?

AUSTIN MACAULEY PUBLISHERS
LONDON * CAMBRIDGE * NEW YORK * SHARJAH

Copyright © **John Stanley Dennis** 2024

The right of **John Stanley Dennis** to be identified as author of this work has been asserted by the author in accordance with sections 77 and 78 of the Copyright, Designs and Patents Act 1988.

All rights reserved. No part of this publication may be reproduced, stored in a retrieval system, or transmitted in any form or by any means, electronic, mechanical, photocopying, recording, or otherwise, without the prior permission of the publishers.

Any person who commits any unauthorised act in relation to this publication may be liable to criminal prosecution and civil claims for damages.

A CIP catalogue record for this title is available from the British Library.

ISBN 9781398428065 (Paperback)
ISBN 9781398428089 (ePub e-book)

www.austinmacauley.com

First Published 2024
Austin Macauley Publishers Ltd®
1 Canada Square
Canary Wharf
London
E14 5AA

To Iliseva.
She ran out of time to write her own book (It's a Fijian name).

I thank all the people I have met in life who have stepped out of the box and lived their life their way.

Chapter One

The shouting and yelling went on and on. My parents were at it again – yelling at each other at the top of their voices. I had heard the same argument three or four times a week for 14 years. Never any resolution, just the same abuse over and over.

I had left home once before totally unprepared and spent the day up one of the creeks eating Queensland nuts all day, but as darkness neared, I had no matches or any place to sleep so I had gone home.

I knew I was leaving this time and I lay there making plans.

Next day, when both of them went to work, I caught the village bus to the local town where I knew was an army disposal store. I had been working locally for six months so I had money in my pocket.

Once I was in the store, the array of goods was overwhelming, but I asked for a hammock. When the attendant suggested two waterproofs to cover it followed by a blanket, I figured that took care of sleeping arrangements and turned my attention to a machete and a small knife, then came the army cooking utensils as well as matches, cigarettes, lighter, and fire starters.

I went elsewhere and bought corded fishing line and a box of hooks. Now I had quite a collection so I went back to the disposable store and bought a backpack. Of course, I needed food so I bought six tins of corned beef and a packet of tea. I had to carry all this so I couldn't buy too much and I was used to foraging around the creeks at home.

Back to the army disposable store to buy a water bottle and mosquito net. I think I had it all this time.

Back on the bus, I got the driver to drop me off a mile from the village. I walked home through the bush and stashed my backpack near a log, placing some branches over it.

That night, I waited until everyone was asleep then I slipped out, leaving a note on the table saying,

'Going west to be a drover, can't stand the fighting anymore.'

I was away, into the bush, picking up my backpack on the way. My first destination was the local rifle range which I knew well as I had been shooting there for two years. There was a lunch shed there and I intended to spend my first night there and after two hours of walking I arrived. I rolled my blanket out on the lunch table and with my backpack for a pillow and a few big sighs of relief I was asleep.

The next morning, I was awake at first bird call, packed up and I was off again. I wanted to put distance between myself and home as my mother had threatened to put the police onto me if I ever left.

Mid-morning, I came across a little-used road heading into the hills, so I followed it and after an hour I came onto an abandoned banana plantation. There was an old packing shed so I dumped my backpack there and went looking for bananas. I was lucky and found two small bunches with ripe bananas.

It was time to eat so I lit a small fire, made a cup of tea, and opened a tin of meat to feed well on bananas and canned meat.

I had a sleep then went foraging for anything to find. I found passionfruit and, great blessing! A pawpaw tree with ripe fruit, also an old cane knife used for cutting bananas.

The afternoon was getting on so I decided to stay as I had shelter and abundant food.

Next morning, I was up and away, loaded down with fruit and a cane knife. I walked all day, following timber roads along the ridges while eating my fruit bonanza. Late in the evening I came onto a clearing where they loaded logs so I set up my hammock to stay the night.

I was sitting near my fire when I felt a presence close to me. I sat very still with my eyes swivelling around, then a head came down over my shoulder. It was a mule's head so I sat still then reached up and rubbed his nose, then forehead and ears. Standing up slowly, I kept rubbing his head and neck. He loved it. What was I to do with a mule?

Well, I could ride him or he could carry my pack but I had no rope to control him. I fed him a couple of bananas and as dark was approaching fast I decided to climb into my hammock fully expecting the mule to move on during the night.

Come first bird-call in the morning I opened my eyes to see the mule dozing by my hammock. He was happy to see me awake and after fruit and a cup of tea I was ready to go. Down the road I went, calling to 'Big Ears' to come, and sure enough he came walking along behind me, then catching up to walk beside me.

It was so good to have a companion and I would pat him all day and lean on him and just to get to know him.

Big Ears and I ambled on westward finding banana plantations for food, while on the meat side I caught live porcupines, which are delicious to eat but I was always sad to kill them. Then came my first snake; A large carpet snake was stretched across our path so a quick chop with the machete and his head was gone. Here was an abundance of meat lasting days.

One night on a full moon, we slipped down to a creek I could see and fished, catching four catfish, one eel and a turtle, and so we continued west.

Big Ears lived on grass which was pretty rough on the hills and he thoroughly enjoyed our fishing trips to the creeks where he could eat lush kikuyu grass, but bananas were his favourite.

One day I'm riding Big Ears along a track, half asleep on his back when he comes to a full stop. My eyes pop open, thinking we had run into another human which I was trying to avoid, but there on the track was a Bunya cone.

I was off his back in a flash and with one chop of the machete I cut it in halves, then came the task of getting the nuts out. Looking around I saw several more cones and discovered I was under a large Bunya Pine. I got busy separating the nuts from the segments of the cone, slowly building a pile of nuts beside me.

Occasionally, I would look up, and then there was a black man standing there looking at me.

"Good day," I said. "My name is John."

"Good day," he said. "My name is Alec."

This conversation was going nowhere so I watched him as he started gathering nuts.

We carried on gathering nuts, both of us sitting on the ground busy with our tasks. After an hour, he pushed his nuts into a bag and stood up saying, "Are you hungry, boy?"

"Not now I've got these," I said.

"Well, why don't you come home for lunch," he said.

"As long as I'm not the lunch," I replied.

He smiled at this, waved his arm in a 'follow me' gesture and said, "Come on."

I collected my nuts, hopped on Big Ears and followed him down the mountain to his home.

Home was a neat little cottage with one bedroom, kitchen and veranda. On arriving, a black whirlwind flew out the door full of questions, but upon seeing me and the mule, she actually stopped talking.

Alec said to me, "This is Moira."

She dashed back inside and then shyly reappeared, but you couldn't keep her quiet for long and she was off chattering again. Just as well for Alec and I were no conversationalists and she filled in for us. Alec gestured to put my gear on the veranda.

"Don't you tie up that mule?" he asked.

"No, he just follows me. We are mates, you see," I said.

I was never introduced to 'Mama' and as that was what Moira called her so did I.

Lunch was real meat with roasted veggies, the finest I'd had since leaving home.

After lunch, I was restless and as Alec and Mama settled down to sleep I fetched my fishing pole and knife and headed to the creek, but soon realised I had company as Moira was tagging along and behind her was Big Ears.

In an attempt to stop her talking, I cut her a fishing pole and set it up for her then dug some grubs from a rotten log, showed her how to bait up and toss it in the water. Finally, we were both sitting side by side fishing. It's funny how we will talk to someone younger when we won't talk to adults. Her questions finally got to me and I told her how I had run away from home and my mum had threatened to put the police onto me so I had stayed in the hills while I travelled west to be a drover.

After that, we talked and laughed all afternoon and caught four catfish, Moira catching three of them. Of course, I had to take a ribbing as we walked home about how she had caught the most and I muttered about 'beginner's luck.'

After dinner, I set my hammock up and thankfully fell asleep.

Next morning, Alec indicated that I should stay as he had to go to work. It was back to the creek for me and Moira where she showed me how to find freshwater mussels. We used some for bait and caught catfish, eels and turtles. We had enough so we swam and lazed the morning away.

That afternoon I decided to make a garden. I put Moira to work and we dragged some logs out of the bush and formed a small square, then filled it with leaf mulch from the creek. I sent Moira in to get some pumpkin seeds off Mama to plant in the mulch. By the time that was all done, Alec was back home and the sun was low. Starting gardens was to become a life-long trait of mine.

After dinner, Alec started talking.

"Boy," he said. "I went to town and saw the police today and they told me to tell you that they are not looking for you and that you can now travel the roads."

That was the most talk I ever heard from Alec.

It took a while to sink in and for me to realise that I could travel the roads, which would speed my way westward.

"Thanks, Alec," I said. "I guess I can move on now with no fear of the police."

Well Moira went quiet and then in a little voice she said, "You can't go, John."

"I'll never be a drover if I don't go west," I said.

Moira ran off to her room and I didn't see her till morning when I was packed up and ready to leave. She dashed out the door and flung her arms around me and kissed me on the lips. She nearly succeeded in keeping me there, I can tell you.

So, I rode back up the hill to the Big Bunya Pine and followed the timber road ever westward but this time I took the first turn leading down into the valley below.

Chapter Two

That time in the mountains had done something to me. I had survived storms, snakes and strange noises in the night, I had overcome many fears and most importantly I had found God and learnt to put my trust in him. When you are on your own with no one to help, who do you turn to when your deepest fears arise? There is only the mythical God, but I discovered that when I called on him he answered not in a showy way but quietly, like sending Big Ears to me and leading me to food. This trust in God would stay with me my whole life even though I never entered a church or took to religion.

These days it would be called 'character building' and they have courses where they take people into the bush to learn to survive.

Well, I followed the timber track down to a lovely green valley full of dairy farms. It was summer, the rain had been good and the grass was green. Big Ears loved it. He stopped and started eating so I sat beside him while he topped up on real food.

We were mates you see, not master and servant. I was always an early starter so it was still only mid-morning when we passed the first house, then the second, and no one rushed out and handed me over to the police so I started to relax. Then as I passed the third house a female voice called out.

"Hey, son."

I turned around, ready to bolt, and answered, "Yes?"

"Can you chop firewood?" she asked.

"Only been doing it half my life," I said.

"OK, I'll give you a job if you want it."

"Sure," I said.

I hung my backpack on the paling fence so Big Ears would know I was coming back and followed the lady around the back to a woodpile. She pointed to the axe and said, "I'll leave you to it."

I must say these country people were short on words, but then so was I.

I chopped for two hours and reduced the pile to firewood. I was wondering what to do next when the lady called me up to the veranda and there she had sandwiches, cake and a pot of tea set out for me.

She sat down and started asking where I came from and where I was going, so I told her I had come from the mountains and was going west to be a drover. We sat, ate sandwiches and cake, drank tea and chatted. When I was finished she paid me ten shillings and said to call on the lady two houses down.

You see, I knew nothing about telephones and didn't know she had been ringing around while I worked.

I walked out of there well-fed and with ten shillings in my pocket. I was rich, huzzah! And as happy as Big Ears was with his green grass.

We moved down to the house two doors down and knocked on the door.

"Are you John?" the lady asked.

"Sure am," I said.

I was led out back to the woodpile and another two hours work. This time I got scones and tea plus a packet of sandwiches for later, as well as my ten shillings. As I was leaving she walked out with a khaki shirt and shorts and said, "Here, you need these."

This made me look at myself and yes, I sure looked a bit ragged.

One day on the roads and I had earned one pound, been fed like a king, and had a new set of clothes. I skipped on down the road, whistling, happy as a lark in a wheat field. I found a camp by the creek, put up my hammock and went to sleep in the shade with the water trickling a lullaby.

I woke near sunset, lit a fire, and caught a catfish to go with the sandwiches. After all, I was 14 and a half, and kids like that can eat.

I was brewing my cup of tea the next morning when a lady pulled up in an old car.

"Are you John?" she asked.

This sounded familiar so I said 'Yes' and she asked me up to cut wood. The telephones had been at work again. I ended up doing a full day's work there. I cut wood, dug and weeded gardens, carted manure for the garden and I got sent out to bring in the cows. The bloke was pretty good and I stayed watching him milk and doing bits and pieces. I got three meals as well as one pound ten shillings.

Back to camp and a deep sleep.

That's how it went for the whole week until Sunday, a day on which no one asked me to work – which I found strange for I was willing – but the people all observed Sunday as a day of rest and they left me alone.

I sat under the tree counting my money and I had seven pounds. An absolute fortune for me.

I caught a couple of catfish for lunch and as they cooked a car pulled up. There I was, staring at my biggest fear. A policeman.

"What's your name, son?" he asked.

"John." I replied.

"I need more than that," he said. "A second name."

One morning, after six weeks of milking, Beth came out crying and said her husband had died. I made her a cup of tea and we sat there, side by side, sharing her grief. Then there was a time of police, ambulances and funerals, but I had to keep the milking going and the farm.

When it was all over, Beth bought a cup of tea out and sat on the veranda with me.

"John," she said, "I don't know what I'll do but if you keep milking for a while, I'll work something out."

A week later, she told me the farm was leased to the man next door and he would take the cows over there to milk.

"John," she said. "I don't want you to feel as if you have to move straight away and you have really been good to us so I've decided to give you our flock of sheep. There are 30 Border Leicester ewes and one ram, as of now they're yours. I'll give you a receipt for them. Now, they are due for shearing. The wool is yours and here is the address of the man who shears them. If you like, I'll ring him and see when he can come."

"Yes," I said. "I'd like that."

Two days later, the shearer turned up.

I ran the sheep into the yard. He set up his shearing machine and went to work. He had me putting the wool into a big hessian bag.

He was finished by lunch, loaded the wool on his Ute, then reached out and handed me 150 pounds. In a cloud of dust, he was gone. These country people sure were short of words.

I had been thinking I would have to pay him, instead he gave me 150 pounds! I just stood there, looking at it until Beth walked up and said, "How much did he give you?"

"150," I said.

"He cheated you a bit, but not badly."

I sat on the veranda counting money. I had 100 pounds I left home with, 150 from wool, and 20 I had saved. 270 pounds. I really was rich, huzzah!

Once over my excitement, I realised I now had the responsibility of 30 sheep to care for. How was I to drive them, pen them at night and generally care for them? I was only nearly 15! I wasn't a six-foot hero. I was average-sized, raised in the country with few social skills, but I knew the bush and I could shoot, had been shooting for two years. I was short on words but everyone else seemed to be too, I was intelligent, learnt quickly, and had high marks in school.

I grabbed my fishing pole and went down to the creek, not to fish but to think. The road ran along the creek mostly but I found a grassy bank and sat there, thinking with my line in the water. Did I want the sheep, could I sell them? My mind was in a whirl.

"Hey son, are you John?"

Not again, I thought.

I turned and there was an old bloke in a battered Ute.

"Yes," I said.

"Do you want a permanent job?" he asked.

"What doing?"

"Cutting firewood and splitting posts," he said.

"OK," I said. "But one problem. I have 30 sheep to look after."

He thought for a while then said, "There is an abandoned farm near my camp. The fellow died and there is a fight over the will. You could put them there."

And so, my term with Old Bill started.

I got directions then went back and told Beth what was happening. She was happy for me and gave me a big kiss. That was two kisses I'd had in my life; things were looking up!

At night Bill, would sit at his fire, sipping from a bottle of rum. Neither of us was talkative but if I needed to know something he would always tell me. He was an encyclopaedia of bush lore.

Next day before he left, he showed me how to stake the wallaby hide out to dry. When he left, I went down to the sheep and so the days and weeks passed.

About four weeks later, I went down to the sheep and there was a man there driving in a stake with a 'FOR SALE' sign on it.

"Hello," he said. "I'm Ray, the stock and station agent."

"I'm John," I said.

"Yeah, I've heard about you."

"How much do they want for this farm?" I asked.

"Well," he said. "The house is rubbish, the sheds are rubbish, the land is overgrown with lantana. It's worthless really, but they want 100 pounds."

I couldn't believe my ears. Only 100 pounds!

"I'll take it." I said.

He looked at me.

"Seriously," he said. "You have to be 18."

"I am," I said. "Ask Old Bill if you don't believe me."

"You got the money?"

"I'll get it now," I said. "It's up in camp."

"No, all I want now is ten pounds and the rest in a month."

I signed the paperwork but had to think quickly when it came to birthdate, which, after a quick mental calculation, I wrote as 1936.

He didn't even look at it. Just folded everything up and said, "It's yours. I'll be back in a month to get 90 pounds and I'll give you the papers then."

I did a little jig, hugged Big Ears, ran in circles, then let Big Ears in to enjoy the kikuyu grass. I walked around and it all looked beautiful, talk about rose coloured glasses. Up the back I went and laid in the pool, my very own pool. I was a landowner, I was king of 40 acres!

That night, I told Old Bill. He grunted and asked if I would still be working.

"Of course," I said.

That settled him down and next thing he gave a big smile and said, "Congratulations."

I couldn't wait for lunch and rushed the chopping so we finished early. I borrowed a brush hook off Bill and when he left I went to work on the lantana on my 40 acres. Lantana is easy to demolish, I chose the isolated clumps and one by one down they went. Where they had been I planted kikuyu runners.

I was chopping the lantana away from the house and yard when I came across a fenced vegetable garden. There was some old sweet potato vines and a very sad mandarin tree. Once the lantana was gone I started digging, replanting the sweet potato vines and promising to get seed. Now that I had cleared the lantana back I started looking at the house. There were several holes in the veranda, damp inside from a leaky roof, an old stove in the kitchen, and windows broken but I reckoned I could do something with it.

I went to work cannibalising the sheds to fix the house. Each night, I would chatter to Old Bill, telling him what I had done. He would sip his rum and I would see a little smile now and then. I still shot wallabies for the pot and skinned them, and Bill showed me how to tan the hides with bloodwood sap, so now I had several hides tanning. I was becoming a

hive of industry.

One afternoon, I was chopping lantana when a voice behind me said, "Good day."

I turned and there was Harry the Policeman.

"Good day," I said.

"I hear you're a landowner now," he said.

"Sure am," I said. "Land and stock owner."

"Good on you, son," he said and put his hand out to shake. We shook hands and he said, "I wish there were a few more like you."

Harry and I became friends after that. I would joke with him and he would call me 'The Squatter.'

Once the lantana had been mostly cleared, I began on the house in earnest. I pulled good sheets of iron off the sheds and replaced the broken sheets on the house, always relying on Old Bill to tell me how to do things. Once I started pulling the sheds apart, I found a treasure of tools: a hammer, a saw, pliers, hoes, and shovels so I could return some of Bill's tools to him. There were tins of rusty nails and these I soaked in oil and put to use. After a week the roof was waterproofed so I began on the house, covered the broken window with tin, patched holes and cleaned the stove and chimney and what a miracle! The stove worked.

That night I tried to talk Bill into moving down to the house but he wouldn't move from his camp. It was what he liked.

I moved down, hung my hammock in one of the rooms, lit the fire and made a cup of tea.

I was home.

Work went on. I was at Bill's camp at first bird call and we cut wood, split posts with me getting half of what we earned.

While all this was happening, the sheep weren't asleep so one afternoon I went down and there was a little lamb running around. I got so excited I raced up to tell Bill and he started to tell me what to do.

After several lambs had been born, I found a new-born lamb with his eyes missing. It was terrible. Up to Bill with the story and he told me that crows peck their eyes out so they'd die and then the crows would have a feed. That, to me, was absolutely cruel. I reached for my rifle and went shooting. No crow was safe, but they are smart birds and after I had shot a couple they'd leave the area. But I always carried my rifle and if a crow came within range he died.

Now, my ram wasn't separated from the ewes so lambs were likely to appear at any time. Bill told me about separating the rams from the ewes and that I had to get a new ram every now and then.

All this knowledge I took on but it was not practical at the moment so the sheep kept doing what sheep do.

I had my first case of fly-blow. That is, blowflies laying maggots in damp wool and this would distress the sheep enormously until I got some hand-shears and cut them out. Horrible job.

One Sunday, I was fed up with working. I had a dry home and the sheep were quiet so I hopped on Big Ears and rode up to see Beth. She was so happy to see me and laid on tea and scones and we had a rare old chat. She told me all the gossip, how Old Bill would brag about me down the pub and the ladies of the C.W.A. had put another parcel of clothes together for me. Most of them I had cut wood for, even Harry was telling the young blokes they should be more like me. I sounded like a celebrity but when Beth described me as a ragged kid riding a mule without a bridle, coming out of the hills and then getting sheep and land and creating a home it seemed to sound different to the way I saw it.

I saw it a bit as desperation and opportunity. I had to work to survive, then Beth herself gave me the sheep and Old Bill and Ray had put me onto the property. Where the locals saw a rundown 40 acres, I saw a home and feed for my sheep.

Beth was doing okay on the lease money and she was seeing a new man so I hoped it all worked out for her. After lunch, we started to wind down a bit so I hopped on Big Ears to go home, promising to come again.

I was 15 now, I had been with Old Bill for nine months, and I had barely been to town except to buy my rifle. Bill bought spuds and onions in town, my garden supplied the other vegetables and my rifle supplied plenty of meat although the wallabies were getting a bit scarce. Bill taught me how to make damper so we lived mostly on our stew and damper. It's called a paleo diet these days and yes, you won't get fat on it.

As time passed, Old Bill did less and less. I started using the chainsaw, cutting the rounds and splitting them into firewood. Bill would still deliver and come back with his rum. Then one day he asked me to deliver the wood but I couldn't drive so an intensive learn-to-drive course was initiated and

I began delivering.

Bill told me where to go.but remember, I was only 15.

One day Harry stopped me and asked me what I was doing.

"You need a license to drive," he told me. "And you can't get that until you are 17."

I told him Old Bill was crook and I had to do it, so I got a stern warning not to drive in town. So, I had to walk into town to buy Bill's bottle of rum. You couldn't do that now, me being underage and all, but they all knew me and the publican would hand the bottle over. They all knew I was now looking after Bill in his old age.

I made the damper and the stews and sat around the fire keeping Bill company. I still went to my house to sleep and tried everything to get Bill to move but he wouldn't. He loved his bush and open-air living. He would say it was bringing the outdoors in.

The wood business was dying as electricity was moving up the valleys one by one and the slow combustion stoves were being replaced by electric ones. I was now only doing about three loads a week.

One evening after eating our stew, Old Bill produced an Arnott's biscuit tin all wrapped in oiled canvas to keep it dry and asked me to care for it, to keep it hidden, and got a promise out of me not to tell anyone for some shyster lawyer would probably cheat me out of it.

Next morning, he sent me off to see such a lawyer and to tell them to go up and see Old Bill. The lawyer arrived the next day and he and Bill talked awhile and shuffled papers around, then off he went.

Several mornings later, I arrived at camp and Old Bill wasn't up so I lit the fire and put our morning stew on to re-heat. Still Bill did not stir so I ducked under his canvas to wake him and that's when I realised everything had changed. He was dead.

I walked back to the fire in a daze and had my last breakfast with Bill.

This was a new experience for me. I didn't know what to do. I decided Harry would know so I drove to Boonah in the Ute to tell him. I drove into town for the first time and stopped in front of the police station. I went in and Harry says to me, "What brings you to town, young Squatter?"

Doing everything I could to hold back the tears, I told him, "Old Bill is dead and I don't know what to do."

He could see I was on the verge of tears and said, "Okay, son. I'll take care of it. You drive back up to camp and keep the birds off him and I'll be up shortly."

The thought of crows pecking Bill's eyes out got me back to camp in a hurry. Harry and an ambulance arrived soon after and carried Bill's body away.

I was at a complete loss.

I made a cup of tea and sat at the fire.

The world had ended.

My job, my teacher, my father had just gone.

He had taught me how to build, to care for sheep, to bake damper, to split posts, chainsaw-work and how to drive. I was devastated.

After a time, I went back to my house, climbed into my hammock and slept. I was in shock but didn't know it.

Harry arrived in the afternoon to tell me the funeral would be in two days' time. I rode Big Ears down for the funeral and when it was over the lawyer approached me and asked me to go to his office. Beth came up to me as well and asked me to visit so I said I would after I had seen the lawyer.

The lawyer told me I was the beneficiary of Bill's will and that after funeral expenses I would inherit 1000 pounds and all of Bill's tools, the Ute, and any personal items.

I was dumbfounded and rode up to Beth's place with my head in a whirl. Beth had lunch ready and afterwards we sat on the veranda together, only this time it was me grieving.

I told her what the lawyer said but I still didn't know what to do. She told me to go back to camp and move all of Bill's possessions down to my house or people would thieve it all.

Next morning, I loaded the Ute with Bill's tools and boxes and moved it all down to my house. All that was left were the poles that Bill had his canvas stretched over.

I was still grieving but the daily tasks got me going again: food had to be cooked, sheep tended, gardens weeded, but I knew a new phase of my life was coming. I had to think.

Out came the fishing pole and down to the creek we went. I sat with my line in the water and let my mind settle. Was I to stay or go? Sell the sheep or keep them? No. I definitely wanted to keep the sheep. I had about 70 now including lambs and it was shearing time again.

I didn't need all the tools so I would sort them and keep what I needed and sell the rest. The Ute had to be sold as I had no license and Harry might stop me driving now that Bill was gone. Would I sell the property or stay? The property was close to overstocked now so I couldn't expand. The money from the sheep was barely enough to support me so unless I sold I was in a poverty rut.

After catching two fish, I had decided to keep the sheep, sell the property, sell the Ute and the tools I didn't want and carry on westward looking for more land. I needed a couple of pack horses and another one to ride, as well as Big Ears.

Next day, I loaded the Ute with the tools I didn't want and drove to the second-hand store, sold the tools there. Never got much but they were mostly out of date and electric tools were taking over. Now the Ute. While I stood pondering, a man walked up and said, "John, do you want to sell the Ute?"

Everyone knew I was underage.

"Yes," I said.

"Would you take 150 pounds for it?" he asked.

"Yes," I said, and so we went to his bank and he handed me 150 pounds.

Now I had to find horses. I walked up to Ray's stock and station agency and asked if he knew of any horses for sale and that I would sell my land if there were any buyers.

"Are we going to lose you, young Squatter?" he asked.

"Yes," I said. "I'm going to continue my journey west. Thanks to Old Bill, I'm better equipped mentally and physically."

He bent back in his chair and tapped the desk with a pen. Finally, he said, "There's a gypsy down at the river crossing selling six horses and a gypsy van. Go and see him. He's bought a bus and wishes to move on."

I walked down to the river crossing, saw the horses and van and wandered over. A man approached and said, "What do you want, son?"

"I'm looking to buy three horses," I said. "But I wanted riding horses, not draught horses."

The horses were like small draught horses, heavy footed, hair hanging from their knees, long manes and tails. It was a time when horses were going out of fashion and cars were
moving in.

"I'll give you all the horses and the van for 300 or so," the dickering started.

While we talked, a girl about my age came overlooking very sullen then started yelling at her dad that he couldn't sell the horses. He pushed her away, then Harry pulled up in his police car and sat there watching the scene.

The girl was punching her dad, the policeman sat watching and I kept insisting I only wanted three horses. He 150 pounds out of my hand and yelled, "Marcia, give this boy a receipt." This was handed out the bus window. The gypsy grabbed his daughter by the scruff of the neck and threw her into the bus, locked the door, ran to the driver door before the girl could escape and drove off.

Harry walked over and asked, "What was that all about?"

"Well, I wanted three horses. The girl didn't want him to sell them. He wanted 300. I had 150 and you were sitting there watching! I think it all got too much for him so he took my 150 and left. Now I have six horses and a gypsy van when I only wanted three horses."

"Well, you got a bargain," Harry said.

"Will you book me for driving without a license?" I asked.

He smiled and said, "Can you drive a wagon?"

"No."

He looked at me and said, "Come on, I'll show you."

Harry helped me harness up two horses, tied the others to the back, then gave me a quick lesson in driving and showed me the brake.

He told me that when I was going downhill, I had to put the brake on to stop the wagon running up on the horses.

"I won't book you today," he said. "As you are a learner driver."

I very tentatively slapped the reins on the horses rumps and wonder of wonders I discovered they knew more than me. The horses took me home with me working the brake and steering them onto the right road.

My poor little farm was getting crowded with 70 sheep and now six horses. One, I discovered, was a stallion so there would be more horses before long. I petted and played with them and finding that they liked humans I hopped onto one's back and he didn't mind.

A couple of days after catching up on bits and pieces, I remembered Bill's tin he had given me. Curiosity won out so I pulled the tin out of hiding and unwrapped it. I lifted the lid slowly and there staring at me was rows of bank notes. I was dumbfounded. I cautiously took some out and started to count. As I got further down there were 50-pound notes and 100-pound notes. When I had counted it all I had

15,000 pounds.

I couldn't believe it.

Now I knew why I had to keep it hidden, for if anyone knew a 16-year-old had 15,000 pounds they would cheat me out of it, accuse me of theft and all sorts of things. I stacked it back in, wrapped it up, and hid it again.

I needed a cup of tea after that so I sat sipping tea, watching a storm build in the southwest, when I saw a flicker of movement near the horses. I watched and waited then I saw a girl moving amongst them.

I went over and asked, "What are you doing?"

"They are my horses," she said.

"No. They're mine," I said. "And I have a receipt and if you take them the police will deal with you."

She collapsed so I carried her into the house.

"How long since you've eaten?" I asked.

"Three days," she said.

So, I went to the stew pot on the stove and got her a plate of food. She ate like a hungry wolf so I followed up with a slice of damper and treacle and a cup of tea. When that was finished, she fell asleep.

I recognised her as the gypsy girl and that's what I called her from then on. I covered her with a blanket and as the storm was brewing and beginning to thunder, I curled up in a blanket too.

An hour or so later, the storm broke and lightning sizzled and thunder seemed to fall on the house. All the devils of hell had been let loose! Amongst all this the gypsy girl crawled into my blanket and we hung onto each other expecting to get blasted any minute.

It passed, thank God, and that was when something awakened between the girl and me. We discovered why men and women are made differently. We discovered it so well that it took the bleating and neighing of animals to get us up at lunchtime the next day. I rushed out, let the animals out to feed, and to make lunch for us.

After lunch, I took Gypsy up to the rock pool and we bathed, swam, and lay in the sun till sunset, then I had to gather the animals and lock them up.

A period of relaxation followed. We made love, we swam, we lay in the sun, we were like two nature spirits enjoying what we had. I think Gypsy even forgot her horses for a while.

All things change and one morning there was a knock on the door and there was Ray standing there asking, "You still want to sell?"

Well, I was having such a good time I blurted out a price that I thought would scare anyone.

"Yes," I said. "For 500 pounds."

Ray said, "Let's make it 600."

Gypsy came out to see what was happening so I introduced her to Ray. Everyone in town would know that I had a girl by afternoon.

"Good," Ray said. "I'll be back this afternoon with the papers to sign. You will have a month to pack and leave."

That town really looked after me and I am forever grateful for their friendship and help.

Chapter Three

It was thinking time again so while Gypsy got to know her horses again, I sat down to figure money. I had 100 pounds in the bank, a 1000 pounds inherited, 600 from the land, 50 from the original wool and the sheep needed shearing again. That would be another 300 pounds plus the wages I saved in a tin for expenses.

So that was 2050 pounds which would be in the bank plus my saved wages which I would keep for expenses. I had a rifle, 70 sheep, six horses, and a gypsy van. I had arrived in the valley with 100 pounds and a mule for a mate, and now I was 16 years old.

Next question. Where to go? What to do? West was the only answer to where, and what to do, well, I had sheep to drove. Also, there was Gypsy. What did she want? So, I called her in and told her I would be moving west again and asked what she wanted to do.

The answer was simple.

"I'm staying with the horses," she said.

I would have to get used to coming second to the horses but I had an ace: I owned the horses.

Life returned to normal. I shot our meat, used veggies from the garden, but now I had to buy flour, potatoes and onions. I kept tanning hides. I had 30 tanned hides and some in an old milk can still tanning.

I decided we would move into the van now to learn to live in it. Gypsy didn't have to, of course, but I did. Then began a week of packing clothes in the van, sorting tools and how to carry them.

The van had its own water tank. We moved into the van, scratching around like old hens until we had it right. We were ready to go but had three weeks to wait. I also moved Old Bill's tin in, building a special hiding spot where people would have to smash something to find it.

The horses were beautiful and quiet to ride so we rode up to see Beth one day. I introduced Gypsy to Beth and we had the usual cup of tea and scones while we chatted. As we were leaving, Beth held me back and whispered, "I like her."

On the way home, I called on the shearer and he arrived the next day, set up his machine and away we went. I did the catching and dragged the sheep out to him, and it went well so we were finished by mid-afternoon. He handed me 300 pounds and off he went.

I knew by now that a bale of wool was worth 1000 pounds so he was doing well but he did the shearing and selling and if I did my own selling I would have to start paying tax. This way I got my cash and all was well.

There was more time to fill in so it was on the horses and off to see Alec. I knew all the timber roads by now so we followed the ridge till we came to the Big Bunya Pine then down to Alec's cottage. On arriving, we slipped off the horses as we always rode bareback then Moira flew out the door yelling, "It's John, it's John!" and flung her arms around my neck. Mama came out to chase her inside but she danced around on one leg.

We finally made it inside to an endless cup of tea and damper. "Here's the fisherman," Alec said, then continued to tell us how Moira had become an avid fisherwoman and they had lived on fish and pumpkin for ages after I left. Moira dragged me outside to see her gardens. She had three now, full of vines of sweet potatoes and beans.

After lunch, we left and I thanked Alec once again for his help. I told him we were moving on and may not see him again but would always remember him.

The day came and the next adventure began.

We drove down to the river at Boonah and camped there. Problem. How to hold the sheep at night. I went up to Ray's stock and feed place and he pointed to an electric fence and battery.

"Good idea."

I dipped into my savings and bought it. I would carry the battery under the van on a shelf I had built to carry tools. I would just have to charge it at each town. Also, I had to stock the van with food. Tinned meat, potatoes, onions and Gypsy added dried peas and beans as well as dried apple and fruit. Also flour and other bits and pieces. At the last minute we bought a road map.

That night we sat around our campfire when a cyclist pulled up and asked if he could use our fire. "For sure," we said and poured him a cup of tea. Out came the army cooking gear and in no time he had two egg and bacon rolls made.

I asked him where he was going and he promptly told us he was off to the Lockyer Valley to pick onions. Gypsy and I looked at each other and decided that was our destination.

Following further talk, he showed us the generator on the front wheel of his bike and said we could put one on each of our four wheels and charge our battery, then we could have light at night. It was a good idea which we put into practise while in the Lockyer Valley. We were learning. Next morning, we were choosing back roads leading to the Lockyer Valley.

Two days on the road, I was driving the van and Gypsy had the stock when I came on a woman sitting beside the road crying her eyes out and a young girl of seven leaning on her back trying to comfort her.

I pulled up.

"Can I help you?" I asked.

She snarled at me, "No. You're a man. You can't help."

I parked the van, hopped on the riding horse and trotted over to Gypsy and told her the situation, sending her over to deal with it.

It turned out that she had been thrown out of her rental house and the bloke had kept all her possessions and raped her for the back rent.

Gypsy got her in the van and we intended to drop her off at Gatton Police Station. Gypsy had to drive. She cried all day in the van but that evening she came out red-eyed and sniffing so we gave her a cup of tea and later a feed of stew and damper. The girl came out then and we fed her as well. The lady said her name was Mary and her daughter was Emily. She never talked about her past again.

Three days later, we came to the Lockyer Valley and fields of onions. I was wondering how to get started when a Ute pulled up and the farmer asked if we wanted work picking.

"Sure do," I said. "But we need a place for the animals."

"Use that lane there," he said. "No one else does."

So, we parked at the front of the lane, turned the sheep in and put up the electric fence. I offered to take Mary and Emily into Gatton on the horses but she wanted to
stay and work.

Our onion picking had started.

When one farm finished we were passed on to another. We got a reputation as hard workers so the work kept coming. Emily had looked out for the sheep while we worked so when we finally got a break I put Emily on Big Ears and we rode to town. I took her to the dress shop and told them to fit her for two pairs of jeans, two shirts, a country hat as well as a pair of elastic-side boots plus undies. Emily came out loaded and while I paid she skipped around in her new gear. I went to the stock agent and he told me of a paddock I could rent for the animals so we took them there and that left us free to work.

Mary and Gypsy had gone to town as well and they both came back fitted out for working and travelling. We ended up working for six months picking all kinds of vegetables.

One day Gypsy came back from town with a guitar. I had no idea she could play but she was very good. That guitar changed our lives. The gypsy van was well-known and people would pull up to talk and pat the horses, but now add a campfire at night and music. The other pickers would drift in, some with instruments of their own, and the dancing would start. We would have a great time but as we were all working it would generally wind down before midnight.

The horses which I had seen has heavy-footed scrubs when I first saw them now shone like the sun. They were all multi-coloured and

Gypsy washed them and brushed them till they shone in the sun. She combed their manes and tails which grew long and glowing and now they were a picture to behold. They were also very loving with humans and people would stop just to see the horses.

On our days off, when a few pickers gathered for yarns and music, Gypsy would put on a riding show. The horse was trained to canter in a circle then with a running jump Gypsy would mount and stand on the horse's rump while it cantered in a circle, then would somersault backward and forward on their backs, hang under their necks, and jump off and on. It was an incredible show of acrobatics and we would all cheer. I began to understand why she didn't want to be parted from the horses.

One night she said, "John, I want to thank you for making all this possible." I gave her a kiss for she certainly brightened up my life, me being a bit of a homebody.

Mary and Emily had worked along with us and Emily and Big Ears were firm friends. She would roll around on Big Ears like Gypsy did on the horses. If she fell off, Big Ears would look around as if to say, "Are you alright?"

Mary had settled in to doing a lot of camp-work while we tended the animals. When the work came to an end and we were preparing to leave, I asked her if she wanted to stay here or come with us.

She looked at me and said, "John, this is the only place I have ever felt love and security and that is worth more to me than anything else."

I was a bit dumbfounded. Here I was, a 16-year-old kid trying to be a drover and by doing that I seemed to be doing all this other stuff.

I figured we were now a family of strays. Big Ears, me, Gypsy, Mary and Emily all having left society to seek our fortune on the road.

We made one other friend in the Lockyer Valley, we called him Bob the Truckie. I think he was sweet on Mary but she didn't want to know. Bob was hauling fruit and vegetables to Brisbane and whenever he could he stopped by to have a cuppa and chat or listen to music.

Chapter Four

We left the Lockyer Valley travelling north up the Brisbane valley. We had considered going up the range, through Toowoomba, but figured the animals may cause traffic chaos and we had heard of work around Kingaroy.

It took us nearly three weeks to reach Blackbutt. We took back roads and travelled slowly to give the sheep a good feed. We took a back road up the mountain to Blackbutt.

We fell into travelling mode and the rifle came out again as we were in wallaby country. Mary was a bit horrified the first time but she got used to it.

Along that stretch we caught up to Mary one day. She was talking to a farm lady. We kept moving and when Mary passed us again there were three hens in a cage hanging on the back. This was becoming a circus, not a droving trip.

We took it leisurely and lessons were learned.

One morning, I crumbled up some damper and fed the crumbs to some apostle birds who live in families. They were feeding happily when a magpie flew in and started bossing them around, chasing them off the feed, then I saw something that taught me a valuable lesson.

Five apostle birds lined up wing to wing like an army and marched on the magpie. The magpie freaked out and flew off.

"Did you see that?" I asked the girls. "They showed us how to deal with bullies. If we stick together we will be right."

That day, I carried my machete and cut four walking stick sized saplings, cut them to length, and that night around the fire I embedded nails in the end of them, protruding about half an inch. They were long enough to hurt but not do serious damage. We called them bully sticks and always kept them handy at night.

In our travelling, we met many great people but there was always an idiot who yelled, "Gypsy bastards!" among other things as they drove past. Now we were ready for them if they stopped.

Also, on this stretch I shot my first deer so we had venison for four days. I prefer wallaby.

When I think back, our hygiene was terrible. I would skin the animal on the ground, cut off the legs and back straps, these we would hang in the van, and they would last three to four days before going off.

Personal-wise we washed when we had a supply of water which wasn't always but no one ever got ill. I think sometimes we can be too clean.

We were camped at a spring one night and when we got up there was a little foal standing by his mum. Gypsy went ballistic, hugging the mum and the foal. We all gathered around them congratulating the mum. We stayed a day to let them regain their strength and then set off for Kingaroy as fast as possible. We could see that another couple of mares were due to have foals.

On getting to Kingaroy, I rented a paddock for the animals and we went looking for work.

It was winter and there was no casual work and as we wanted to give the mares time to have their foals we went looking for other work. Gypsy and I got work at the bacon factory but Mary wouldn't go in and she wandered off. That night she told us she had work in a cafe so we all settled down to regular work.

We didn't like it but a second foal convinced us we were doing the right thing.

I turned 17 there and we splashed out and went to a cafe for a meal. I had never eaten in a cafe so Mary took over and showed us what to do. That seems strange now in a time of fast foods and people basically living on that food but times have changed rapidly.

After two months, we had five foals and more lambs. We now had 160 sheep. Those lambs kept on coming.

One evening, we sat around the fire, each one of us with our gloomy thoughts, then we all burst out at the same time, "Let's leave."

We looked at each other and burst out laughing. Obviously the settled life was not for us.

Emily had been at school and when we said we were leaving she burst into tears of joy, but this time Mary joined her up in a correspondence course, the lessons being sent to the next town on our way.

Three days later, we left. We now had quite a herd of animals and we pushed them a bit till we got off the main road, turning into the Dalby road heading west.

It was winter with cold winds and Mary pulled the tanned wallaby hides out and started making us leather coats. Emily first then Gypsy and I had to be measured and fitted each night. Mary had bought the needles and thread in Kingaroy and before long we were all outfitted with wallaby skin coats which stopped the wind beautifully. Next came knee high moccasins for me and Gypsy for we often got sweat sores on our legs from riding bareback. They were a luxury, I tell you. Then came belts, circles to pull their hair up in and anything else she could think of.

Wallabies were thick here so I was shooting meat again and gathering hides. We tanned them in a milk can, tied on the side and the lid sealed to keep the smell in. That was my job. Mary did most of the camp work, I would set up the electric fence and lastly Gypsy would bring in the stock.

We camped at the Stuart River for a few days and people would pull up to see the horses. The children loved the foals. If Gypsy had the guitar going people would stay and listen.

That's how it went and one evening a truck stopped and the truckie came strolling over.

"Are you John and Gypsy?" he asked.

"Sure thing," we answered.

"Well Bob has been on the blower asking if any truckies had seen you. He wants to know how you're going."

"Next time you're talking tell him we are doing very well. We now have 11 horses and 170 sheep plus three hens and a Mary and Emily."

"He has asked us to keep an eye on you in case there is any trouble."

We fed the truckie cups of tea, damper and stew. He loved it and Gypsy gave him a tune to send him off. Well, that started our association with the truckles. They would pull up regularly, get a cup of tea and a feed if there was any. We never knew what was said over the air but it suddenly seemed that every truckie was our friend.

They saved us from an incident one night. Two men had pulled up and came up to the fire. We gave them tea but we didn't like them. Our bully sticks were on the ground behind us. Then they started telling crude jokes to the women and making offensive remarks suggesting that I couldn't keep two women happy and that they had better help me out. I saw Mary reach for her bully stick, then the rest of us had our hands on our own and things were about to get ugly when the squeal of brakes announced a truck stopping. A big red headed truckie wandered over.

"Got a cuppa?" he said.

We poured him a cup. He could feel the tension and asked if we were alright.

I said, "No, we're not. And these men are about to leave."

The truckie turned around, smashed a fist into one fellow's face and kicked the other in the groin.

"Now listen good, you blokes. Us truckies look after these kids and you'd better leave them alone."

That was the end of that. We fed the truckie our best and he drove off. We called him Big Red and we were to hear of him again. Big Red taught me a good lesson. If you're going to get violent, don't waste time on threats and arguments. Just do it.

We moved on ever westward and reached Durong then on past heading for Chinchilla. Gypsy and I drove the stock. Mostly I drove the stock while Gypsy did somersaults on the horses. She was always coming up with new tricks. I learnt some. I could stand upon their rumps and do a couple of somersaults but never with the smoothness Gypsy had.

One day I went into the van for lunch and was quietly munching away when Gypsy arrived at a gallop.

"John! John! There's a big dog in the sheep."

I grabbed my rifle, leapt on the horse and away we went. I was picturing dead sheep and blood everywhere, but when we arrived the sheep were eating along, calmly.

"Where?" I asked.

"There," Gypsy said, pointing. Sure, enough there was a big white dog in the middle of the sheep. I watched him. She just stood there looking about, then I noticed that there were Merinos mixed with the Border Leicester.

I did a rough count and there were about 50 extra sheep. On closer inspection, I saw the dog had long ringlets hanging in her coat for she was full of burrs and grass seed and also looked quite thin. She appeared to be guarding the sheep so we left her alone and kept the drove going. She just moved along with the sheep. Another 50 sheep would be good but we weren't thieves so we would have to report this.

That evening we drove the sheep in and the dog came as well. Once the sheep were penned the dog sat down beside them. She was thin so I got our spare leg of wallaby and tossed it to her. She started chewing immediately. She was a mess of burrs and grass seed.

We were sitting around after dinner, Gypsy playing her guitar, when I noticed the dog silently approaching Emily.

I said, "Don't get a fright, Emily, but the dog is coming up to you. Just sit still and see what she does."

The dog crept up, step by step, then touched Emily with her nose.

"She has said, 'hullo Emily now turn and rub her ears and head,'" I said. And that was the beginning of a firm friendship.

I tossed Emily a pair of hand-shears and suggested she get the horse brush and went to work on the dog. After an hour she was looking more like a dog and she was licking Emily's face.

Gypsy made up a song about Shaggy the dog and so she became known as Shaggy.

A police car regularly patrolled the road so next day I waited and pulled him up, telling him of the dog and sheep and could he find out who owned them. I told him how uncared-for the dog was.

"OK," he said, and drove off.

Two days later, he pulled up and said the dog had been owned by an old chap who'd died. He had used the dog to guard his sheep but no one had seen the dog for six months. She must have stayed with the sheep and been forgotten. He said to keep the dog and the sheep as everything had been settled long ago.

So, we acquired another stray. We were certainly a band of strays.

A bond developed between Shaggy and Emily. When she wasn't with the sheep she was lounging beside Emily. Emily fed her, brushed her, and laid all over her using her as a pillow. Shaggy took it all and would give her a good licking. If she had scratches then Shaggy would lick them clean. It looked like a life-long friendship had formed.

If Emily forgot to brush her, she would pick up the brush and drop it in front of her.

On westward we went till we came to a fork in the road, one to Dalby the other to Chinchilla. There was a good campsite so we stopped. It had rained recently so there were puddles for the sheep.

We'd settled down for the night, had dinner, and out came the guitar.

Then a car pulled up and out got four men all holding something!

The sense of danger was immediate so we reached for our sticks and moved away from the fire and stood shoulder to shoulder. I was on one end, Mary and Emily in the middle with Gypsy on the other end, then Shaggy pushed in beside Emily and Big Ears quietly moved up beside Gypsy.

The men approached and we saw they had guns. Scary! But we stood still.

They didn't muck around. One of them said, "We are here for the girls so you might as well come good or there'll be trouble."

What followed took no more than a minute but longer in the telling. I will call them Number One, Two, Three and Four, with Number One being opposite me.

Number Two reached for Emily and grabbed her wrist, saying, "I'll start with the little one."

Shaggy jumped forward, grabbed his arm, bit down hard and shook. I could hear the bones breaking. Number One started to lift his shotgun to shoot the dog so I slammed my stick down on the barrel which knocked it down and he pulled the trigger, blowing off half his foot. He started to raise it again so I hit his arm this time and heard the bones break, then I cracked the stick across his nose as hard as I could. He fell backward.

I looked up. Shaggy had her man down and was going for his throat but he had got his other arm up in time so Shaggy was biting on his arm and face. Mary, not wanting to be raped again, slammed her stick down on Number Three's head, fracturing his skull as we found out later. He just stood there. Stunned.

Number Four had reached for Gypsy but Big Ears bit down on his arm and flung him backwards dislocating his shoulder and causing him to drop the rifle. Big Ears then spun around and started kicking with both hind legs at once. Number Three was still stunned and next thing there were mule hooves flying all around him. One broke his jaw; another sent his rifle flying and it discharged when it hit the ground. More hooves slammed into his ribs and belly, breaking four ribs doing the insides damage.

Number Four was recovering and getting up and reaching for his rifle. Big Ears dashed over and began hammering his chest with his front feet. The four men were down and I could see that Big Ears was going to kill the fellow so I dashed over, slammed into Big Ear's shoulder, and knocked him sideways. Big Ears was in a fighting mood and he spun about, ready to start kicking me, but I was shouting his name and he stopped in time.

They were all down and in a bad way. I put a halter on Big Ears and tied him up, then looked around to see Mary and Emily pulling Shaggy of her victim. Shaggy sat back, growling and barking. What to do now? We had four badly injured men!

Just then I heard a truck coming so I dashed out to the road and waved him down.

"Will you call the police and an ambulance?" I asked. "There are four badly injured men over here."

The truckie got on his blower and called them, stressing the urgency.

The truckie walked back over with me and said, "My God! What happened here?" and walked around checking the men. They were all feeling the pain now, crying and moaning, asking for help. I gave the truckie a very brief account of what happened. There wasn't much we could do or wanted to do for them so we checked each other and everyone was okay so we waited for help.

Then we heard the sirens and two police cars and four ambulances began arriving, one by one. The ambulance men went to work, with me explaining what had happened to each man. Number Four was the worst, with multiple broken ribs. He could hardly breathe. He got rushed off first. The others were in no immediate danger so they got bandaged up and sent off. It was time for the police, so we told our story with it all coming out in a rush from four people. They slowed us down, got us to have a cup of tea, and then questioned us one at a time till they had a good idea of what had happened.

I stressed to them that I didn't want anything to happen to the dog or the mule because they had saved the girls from rape and had possibly saved their lives.

Another car had pulled up and it was the farmer from a half mile up the road. He had heard the shots and then the sirens so he came down to see what was happening. The truckie had filled him in on what he knew and now he came over and we gave him a cup of tea. Phillip was his name, but shock was setting in and we started laughing hysterically with the comments like, "Did you see his face, and Shaggy shaking and chewing, Big Ears throwing men around?" and so on. It took a while but we calmed down again and then we could Wtalk sensibly.

We had told the police we would stay put for a couple of days so we slept in and then got up to make breakfast. Phillip drove in so he got a cup of tea and after a chat he asked if we wanted work. We said yes, but we needed a paddock for our own sheep and horses.

"No worries," he said. "There is 500 acres fenced.

You can put them in there."

"Right then, we will move up later," I said.

Phil then explained how he was clearing 2000 acres for grain and he needed help picking up sticks, ploughing and seeding.

We moved up during the day and set up a camp near his windmill for water and left behind a notice tacked to a tree saying we had moved a half-mile that way.

We began work for Phil and Susan, his wife and daughter, Jazmin. Jazmin was the same age as Emily so an immediate friendship developed as they were both lonely for company their own age. Susan took Jazmin to school each day so she enrolled Emily as well and that took care of Emily.

The police arrived again, checking up on details and told us that the men had been charged with attempted rape, assault with a deadly weapon, and a few other things. The trial would happen in a month when they got out of hospital.

Number Four was in a critical condition but was expected to survive.

"By the way, as part of the investigation we looked up your dog. He is a Great Pyrenees Mountain Dog and they have been guarding sheep for thousands of years, obviously they guard humans too. There is a man breeding them in Toowoomba," he said.

Phil and Susan lived in a big shed with one end walled off for living quarters. Susan was struggling with the conditions a bit, and loneliness, and the arrival of Gypsy and Mary was very welcome.

It was time to begin work. Phil was knocking down the bush with the dozer and we came behind with a tractor and trailer picking up sticks. Once that was done we would plough the ground, turning up more sticks, then we would go over it again picking up the sticks. We took turns on the tractor so none of us got too bored. It was winter so the temperature wasn't a problem. We had Sunday off which was my time to ride around the sheep and shoot any crows hanging around. Shaggy guarded the sheep and when Emily and Jazmin came home from school, Emily would catch Big Ears and round up the sheep, penning them for night.

Jazmin had never ridden so it was great to see them riding off double bank while Emily got Big Ears to trot just so Jazmin would bounce around on his back. After a time, they moved onto the horses and would go galloping down the paddock together, laughing and carrying on.

After two weeks, Susan started to come out to help us. We taught her to drive the tractor, laughing and cheering at her jump starts, but she started to enjoy it and talked along with the girls. At lunch she would go in early and prepare lunch for us all. She didn't come out in the afternoon as it was school pick up. Susan did shopping and we made our own meal at nights, then the guitar would come out. It got so two or three nights a week Phil and Susan would come and join us and we would all sing the favourite country songs of the time.

Phil finished the dozing and came behind us ploughing, then when we finished the sticks we had two tractors going discing and harrowing. Phil borrowed a second planter and we had both tractors going, planting sorghum.

One day it was finished, just like that.

We parked the tractors and Phil said, "Time for a beer."

That night Susan invited us over for dinner and as there was dark clouds rolling in we accepted.

The girls were in the kitchen and I was sharing a beer with Phil, when he leant forward and said, "John, I want to thank you for saving our marriage. You have put the life back into us. Jazmin is a different girl, Susan is laughing and talking and can now ride a horse and drive tractors, she has come to accept the bush and realises that there is a lot to enjoy out here. I want you all to stay as long as you want."

"We will move on eventually," I said. "But we would be happy to stay a couple of weeks and rest up."

I was a bit embarrassed so I leant forward and picked up a paper, the 'Country life.' As I did, I noticed the date. The 25th of July. I looked at Phil and said, "You had me working on my birthday. Now I'm 18 and can legally own land."

I told Phil how I was worried about the girls after the attack and I myself was fed up with the droving idea. I would like a home.

We were interrupted by dinner arriving and we all set to it knowing there was no work tomorrow. As we ate, the heavens opened and the rain poured on our newly planted seed. Phil couldn't stop smiling. "With that crop," he said. "I can build a house for Susan."

Next day, I told the girls of my decision to buy a property and if either of them didn't want to stop, or didn't like the place I bought, that they were free to leave. There was a collective sigh of relief and they said, "We thought you'd never stop, you were so keen on droving."

"Phil has asked us to stay on and the sheep are overdue for shearing so I will go to town tomorrow and arrange that first."

I went with Susan on the school run to Jandowae and saw the stock and station agent. He put me onto a shed about 20 miles from us and rang and made the arrangements for the shed and the shearing contractor. I also told him I was looking for land to buy. I wanted good grass country for the horses and water.

Next morning, we were on the road again with the promise of being back in five days. We left some gear behind to lighten the load and only took four horses. We acted as roustabouts, picking up wool and doing the pressing. In a day and a half, it was done and we had seven bales of wool. The stock and station agent came out, branded the bales and said there was a sale in a month's time and we were to stay in touch with him to get our cheque.

We got a day's relaxation in, watching over naked sheep running around, then a police car pulls in and says that the trial will be next week and we must be there as witnesses. Susan offered to run us in on the day.

We lined up, gave our testimony and listened to the police evidence. In the end they were given ten-year sentences and we breathed a sigh of relief.

It looked like we were getting a chance to rest when Phil wandered over with the Country Life newspaper and he said, "There is 1000 acres of grassland in here for 500 pounds, between Warwick and Killarney."

"I can manage that," I said.

"I'll drive you over tomorrow," Phil said.

Everyone wanted to come but the car wasn't big enough. In the end, Susan offered to stay behind and do the school run.

We left early and by nine o'clock we were waiting outside the agent's office. Gypsy was jumping up and down all excited and said she'd had enough of the travelling as a child.

We saw the agent and he drove us out to the block of land. There it was. Beautiful rolling grassland with a creek at the bottom. It was fenced on three sides and the creek was the fourth boundary. The girls were saying, "Yes! Yes!" but I made the agent drive down to the creek. It was full of water. A good fishing and thinking spot. The fences would hold the sheep and there was an old shed and sheep yards there which needed fixing. That was it, except for the big shady gum trees along the creek.

While we sat in the shade by the creek, the agent said, "There's another 1000-acre lease across the creek you can get for a 1000 pounds."

I looked at the girls shining faces and said, "We will have both."

The girls jumped in the air and hugged each other. Phil said, "You'd think they were tired of travelling."

Back to town to sign papers and for me to draw out the 600 pounds from the bank for the deposit. While this went on the girls went shopping as girls do.

It was lunch time so off to a cafe where I shouted everyone a bang-up meal.

Then it was back to Phil's place for we now had a month to fill in before we left and to think about the move. It was a leisurely two weeks. We helped Phil do little jobs, the girls had Susan up on the horses trying to teach her tricks, and Emily and Jazmin galloped all over the place. We watched the little green shoots come out of the ground and begin to grow into a crop. We had music at night and Gypsy was teaching Susan how to play the guitar. It was relaxing and fun.

One night, I dropped the bombshell. How are we going to move? No one wanted to go droving anymore now we had land but that land was 250 miles away. I didn't want to either so I had decided to transport the sheep but that left the horses and wagon. We could probably get the horses there in three or four days but the wagon would slow us. Phil spoke up and said he could take the wagon on his flat-bed truck and the neighbours had a stock crate for the horses, so it was all arranged and we could relax again. The fun went on.

The day came as always, but first I had to recover a certain tin box, so I banged and rattled around in the van till I came up with Old Bill's tin.

Gypsy poked her head in and said, "I knew you had a secret, that boxed tin wasn't there before."

"Well, it's still a secret," I said.

Phil and I towed the van onto the truck and chained it down ready to go. In the morning the neighbours came over and we loaded the horses while the sheep transport man and the girls loaded the sheep.

We were off, huzzah!

It was a bit slow on the journey because of the livestock but three hours saw us there, then the unloading began and went well. We took the wagon down to the creek to unload and as the girls were very practised in camping they had a fire going and a cup of tea in no time. Susan had brought lunch so we celebrated.

Phil had brought a tarpaulin which he set up on the back of the truck for him and Susan to stay the night. We had a great feast which the girls had come prepared for, then out came the guitars to start the singing and dancing. It was a great night and we were very slow in getting up the next day.

I still had to pay for this so I caught a ride into town with Phil and Susan as they were leaving. I had my tin tucked under my arm, you bet.

I went to the agent and counted the money out for him. His eyes bugged out a bit when I opened the tin but he kept his mouth shut. I counted out 5400 pounds for him, got my receipt, and it was done. I was finally home.

I strolled out of the agent's office and there on the next door was a sign saying Financial Manager.

"What's he do?" I asked the agent.

He looked at me and said, "He invests money for people."

"Is he honest?"

"Well, no one has shot him yet," he said.

In I went, passing a large country bloke on the way in.

"What can I do for you, sonny?" he said.

I said, "I've got 10,000 pounds to invest."

His jaw dropped but he recovered quickly and said, "Excuse me," while he dashed to the door and called, "Fred! Come back."

The big country bloke came in and sat down.

"Now, let's get to know each other," he said.

"I'm John," I said and shook hands with Fred. The Agent said, "I'm Michael," and we shook hands all around.

"Now Fred," said Michael. "Tell John the deal."

Fred began by saying that the government has shut down a big sheep station in north South Australia and will add it to the national park. "They paid for the sheep and the owner has left, leaving 20,000 sheep running loose. I have people mustering them, transport lined up and I need 10,000 pounds to pay for it. The sheep will be brought back to this county. I have paddocks arranged to take them. I will give you 5000 pounds on your ten in about eight months."

Now I'm not silly and am good at Maths so I let the numbers run through my head and there was a lot of money here and a little risk.

"If you double the 10,000," and so the bargaining began. It ended up I was to get 5000 pounds and 2000 sheep which was two truckloads of sheep with six-months' wool in eight days. I got them because it made me an accomplice in one big sheep duffing operation and I would keep my mouth shut.

"Let it happen," I said, and we shook hands and signed papers.

I stood up and said, "Just to keep things clear, I'm going to buy a Holden Ute and then I'm going to the police station to get a license."

It was a bit dodgy because the sheep actually belonged to the government but before they got around to doing anything the sheep would be killed by dingoes and thirst. I also realised that an 18-year-old kid with 10,000 pounds in a tin probably looked a bit dodgy so this way all my money could come back to me in a legitimate form. I think it's called money laundering. Even though I carried Old Bill's will with me to explain it, it was not listed in the will. This would put me square with the banks and everyone would stay silent.

I walked up to the Holden agency and bought a Holden Ute. I still had 500 in the tin and had to get the rest from the bank. I sat in my Ute as happy as a bee in a flower and I did some thinking.

I had over 1000 pounds in the bank with a wool cheque of approximately 6000 coming within the month, plus 2000 sheep arriving in eight days. Not bad for a ragged boy on a mule without a bridle.

I walked up to the police station and who was behind the counter but Harry the Boonah policeman!

"Good day, squatter," he said. "What are you doing here?"

"Giving you a chance to book me for no license," I said.

We settled down to a good yarn and he said he had been transferred and I gave him the story of our journey.

Harry said, "I'd heard about the attack on you kids so I rang the boys and gave you a good rap."

When we slowed down I asked if I could get a license for driving.

"Well, I know you can drive," he said and started the process of giving me a license. "You still got that little Gypsy girl?" he asked.

"I haven't got her," I said. "Like the mule she stays because she wants to."

Harry smiled at that. I gave him our address and he promised to call out and see us.

I drove home and the girls swarmed me to look at the Ute. I told them that in eight days, 2000 sheep would arrive and until then I wanted to sleep. I tried to but next morning this car drove in and a man got out and started calling us gypsy bastards and that he would drive us out.

Here I was, home at last, trying to sleep and I'm being abused by this bully. Something snapped in me, all the childhood shouting, the idiots along the road, the attack we had experienced.it all came to the surface and I took a leaf out of Big Red's book, picked up my bully stick, walked up to the bloke and without a word smacked him across the shins, hard. His eyes popped out, he spluttered, backed up to his car and drove off.

"Couldn't have done better myself," a voice said behind me. I looked around and there was a bloke on a horse. "I'm your neighbour," he said. "I came over to say hello."

"Well, hop down. The girls already got the billy on."

We all sat down for a cuppa and a yarn and Mary made scones in the camp oven to go with the tea. Ray was his name and we all shook hands and started to get to know each other.

While we talked, we noticed a police car driving in. Harry got out and said, "What's this, John? Are you getting violent? A man claims you attacked him and nearly broke his shins."

I looked up and said, "He slipped and hit his shins on his car door."

Ray spoke up and said, "That's how it was."

"Case closed," said Harry. "Now pour me a cuppa."

Ray explained how that fellow was a serial pest and everyone wanted him out of the district, unfortunately he lived next door to us.

Ray invited us over for dinner that night and so a firm friendship had started.

When we went to dinner we met Caroline, Ray's wife. Mary was wearing one of her wallaby-hide creations all decorated and Caroline was fascinated. She came over the next day to see the rest of the creations. I left them to it, but that started a partnership that prospered. Mary was a very good craft lady and Caroline could sell an ice cube to an Eskimo. That's how 'Country Creations' started. Mary bought a leather sewing machine, moved it into Caroline's shed, and so a business was born.

Gypsy and I were sitting down the creek with our lines in the water, so I asked her what she wanted to do. "Horses and music," she said.

She drove into Warwick, went to the best pub and offered to play on a Saturday night. She sang for the bloke and he said, "Okay, start this Saturday."

Saturday night we all went in to listen. We sat with a beer in front of us and out came Gypsy. She played and sang all the popular country songs and encouraged the audience to sing as well. As the alcohol loosened the vocal cords, everyone began to sing. She wound up with the whole pub singing Waltzing Matilda.

It was incredible and Gypsy had herself a permanent job and heaps of fans.

The Warwick Rodeo was known all over Australia and it would happen in a month's time. I noticed Gypsy working the horses hard, doing all her tricks and more. When asked what she was up to, she went all secretive and said, "Wait and see."

Then my sheep arrived and I had more to concern me. Suddenly there were 2500 sheep running on 1000 acres. Yes, it was spring and we'd had a couple of storms to bring on a green pick, but I had a moment of depression on how to cope. I sat by the river in a panic and after a while Mary came down and sat with me.

"What's up?" she asked.

"I'm having a panic about how to feed 2000 sheep for six months on a 1000 acres," I said.

We sat for a bit and then Mary said, "That's a forestry over there and it's not fenced. You can feed over the whole forest area. Plus, the storms are coming and that will bring on new grass. Give it a go, John," she said.

Next morning, I hopped on a horse, drove the sheep over the creek and started them feeding on the forest lease and every morning after that for a month, meanwhile at home, acres was regenerating.

Gypsy stopped me one morning and said, "There is enough grass here for a week, John. You must come to the rodeo!"

I agreed so we left Shaggy in charge, piled into the Ute and went off to the rodeo. Unknown to me, Gypsy had already taken some horses in and had arranged to do a riding display in the ring.

At lunch when the action calmed down, out came Gypsy on her two favourite horses and did she put on a show! She rode out standing on both horses, a foot on each rump, then she started jumping from horse to horse, somersaulting, jumping on and off, hanging under their necks and much more. It was a display of horsemanship rarely seen. When she finally stopped the applause was deafening.

Then a chap got on the microphone and said, "What a fine display! That was on quiet horses, but what can she do on an unrideable horse?" He said 'Wildfire' had never been ridden and if Gypsy could stay on his back for ten seconds he'd pay a 1000 pounds.

Gypsy walked up to the microphone and I'm shouting, "No! No!" but she walked up and accepted the challenge. Now Gypsy had a wonderful talent with horses and I often suspected she could communicate telepathically with them. I was about to find out I was right.

Wildfire was in a chute, saddled and ready to ride. Gypsy walked over, climbed the rail and started talking to him. She then asked for the saddle to be removed and put a halter on instead of the bridle, then she let him out of the chute. He came out, snorting and humping his back but Gypsy kept talking and whatever she was doing mentally. Suddenly, she leapt on his back and he bucked in the air, but instead of flying off Gypsy went up in the air with him and when they came down Gypsy was standing on his rump demonstrating with him.

A couple of crow-hops which Gypsy rode with bent knees then she slid onto his back all the time talking to him. The horse fidgeted, a couple more crow-hops and he settled down and began to trot around the ring. Second time around she cantered and then opened him out to a gallop. She pulled up in front of the microphone and called out, "Is that ten seconds?"

Once again, the applause was deafening and Gypsy had made her name as an A1 Horse Handler. The owner wrote out a cheque for 1000 pounds and gave it to Gypsy, then announced she could have the horse as well as his reputation was now in tatters.

Gypsy was to win a lot of races with that horse, but that was to come.

Next day she did another display, then rode Wildfire around the ring at full gallop backward. The crowd loved it and her name was made.

Gypsy went off and bought a truck and stock crate with the 1000 pounds, so we all drove home after a wonderful time.

Gypsy was a celebrity of course and horsemen started arriving with horses for her to quieten or to break in so she became very busy, but for me it was back to the forest with the sheep.

I grazed that whole forest and I noticed that if I moved to a new area each day the grass behind me grew back quite quickly. I was to put this observation to use later on. It was summer and the storms came, then the rain came, the grass grew, I got wet and grumpy, but on we went.

With the 6000 pounds from the wool cheque, I put two carpenters to work to build a two-stand shearing shed near the old yards. I added a large wire holding yard in which I put the sheep each night. That eased my mind and I could get some good sleep.

I never wanted to do six months work like that again, but it achieved its purpose. Shearing time came and we had forty-five bales of wool and the stock and station agent had a buyer for the sheep off-shears. The buyer collected the shorn sheep each day so that when the shearing was finished all the Merinos were gone and I was left looking at my small flock of Border Leicester. I heaved a great sigh of relief and went up to the van for a cuppa and a day's sleep.

While I had been riding the sheep I'd had a lot of time to think and although I originally thought Old Bill's 15,000 pounds was his life's savings, I now thought it may have been earned through some nefarious action, hence the secrecy. But, in respect for Bill's memory I decided it was his life's savings which I had now turned into 40,000.

I never heard anything about a big sheep duffing operation so I assumed Fred had pulled it off beautifully. I was now set up financially and could relax a bit. I told Michael to keep re-investing 15,000 at the best interest he could get as I intended to keep that investment separate from the farm.

While I was totally absorbed in my sheep the girls hadn't been idle. Mary's business with Caroline was keeping them very busy. As Caroline said, she could sell an ice block to an Eskimo, and Mary was developing into a great designer. They now employed an extra lady to do the sewing and Caroline was busy opening a shop in Toowoomba. Mary was doing the designing and decorations on the clothes. The money was rolling in but that was spent on development at the moment.

Gypsy still played at the pub on Saturday night and was extremely popular, as well she was busy breaking horses for people and training them for whatever was needed.

Emily was at school much to her disgust but each school holidays either she would go over to Phil and Susan's or Jazmin would come over to our place. They favoured our place as we had the horses. The foals had grown so I asked Gypsy to break a couple in and I gave them to Phil and Susan so the girls had horses to ride. Phil and Susan also used them as quiet relief from cars. We never bought saddles for the horses as we grew up riding bareback. I guess we looked like a bunch of Indians.

Now the big money was in, I called the carpenters in and started them building a four-bedroom house with verandas and also an outdoor area, concreted and covered by a roof with an open fireplace in the centre. We were still living in the Gypsy wagon which we had pushed into the end of the shearing shed, so we had a bit of cover and a dry floor when it rained.

It had been a hectic 12 months but we were young and healthy, although about every ten days I always felt it necessary for me to take a day off and sleep. That need is still with me, it's been a life-long trait.

Everything happened so fast, lots of small details slipped by us. We now decided to name the place 'The Gypsy Wagon' so I carved a sign for the front gate, then I realised I needed a front gate, not a wire one. In went the posts, the new galvanised gate was erected, and up went the sign. The Gypsy Wagon was born.

What about our garden? I chose a site close to the house, ran the electric fence around it and put the sheep in there each night for a week which fertilised it beautifully. Ray was growing grain so he had all the machinery and came over to plough and cultivate the soil. I went into town and I bought all the fruit trees I thought would grow there and went home to start planting. I made vegetable beds and planted them but of course that required a pump on the river and pipelines.

Eventually it was done and it began to prosper.

We were still living on tin meat and a few fish from the river and the occasional wallaby I shot. While I was doing that, the house was going ahead and I had time to notice that Shaggy had come on heat. This meant a trip to the breeder in Toowoomba. So, the girls came; Mary to visit their shop and Gypsy to shop and look around. We dropped Shaggy off, rented a room at the hotel, and then the girls were off and I could have a quiet beer and a yarn to other country folk.

I was 19 now. I had money, land and stock. Gone were the days when ten shillings made me think I was rich, but life being what it is I thought to myself that those days could come back.

I strolled down to Country Creations to have a look and was amazed at the variety of goods the girls were producing. There was everything from teddy bears and shoes to high fashion clothes. I would have to spend a bit less time with the sheep and take notice of what was happening around me.

We picked Shaggy up the next morning. She had a contented look on her face for she was achieving her life's purpose. We drove home all happy and chatting.

Two weeks later, we were informed that the house was finished with electricity and phone lines attached. We were now part of the world. That required another trip to town to buy beds, furniture, refrigeration and a stove. We all chose to have a separate room as we had been cramped in the van for so long, to have the luxury of space was incredible. Then we unpacked the van into the Ute and moved all our personal belongings up to the rooms.

Life went on, Mary worked in Ray and Caroline's shed, Gypsy was out with the horses, I checked the sheep each day and did the garden which was growing fantastically. I now had time to think about my land and future. How I was I to develop the land and flock and was it all enough to support us? Should I go into grain like Ray? But I had grown to like my sheep.

Six months passed quietly, thank God.

Shaggy had her pups so we had ten squirming pups crawling around. Shaggy fed them and did the looking after while we sat around going, "Oooh!" but it wasn't long before she started taking the pups out to the sheep and we had to count them each night to see that they all came back. A couple of times we had to go and find one or two till they got big enough to keep up with Mum and then we left their training to Shaggy. After all, she knew more about guarding sheep than we did. It was her heritage.

Then one night as I relaxed in my squatters chair — yes, we had graduated — Gypsy came and sat beside me and quietly announced that she was going to leave.

Now every time my life changed, I had given the girls a chance to leave. I didn't want them to feel as if they had to stay and help me.

Gypsy and I had become lovers during the night of that storm so long ago and we had maintained our love making right throughout the journey. After all, we were two young and virile people. I'm sure we told each other that we loved the other but we never discussed marriage or our future. Now we were maturing. Me being 20 years old and she 19 and we had both built a career, Gypsy with her horses and me with my sheep. While I was a homebody, Gypsy was outgoing.

Gypsy had never fallen pregnant which she explained by saying she chewed on a herb her mother had told her of, but she never did become pregnant in the rest of her life so whether she was naturally sterile or perhaps she chewed too much herb I'll never know.

Now she was going to leave. It hit me hard and I couldn't say anything for a time. Gypsy sat and waited and finally I said, "What are you going to do?" she then explained that Wildfire was one hell of a galloper and she was going to go around the country races and clean up, as she put it, and also if I would sell her two favourite horses she would continue with her trick riding.

"I won't sell them to you," I said. "But I will give them to you, and if they aren't pregnant now you can have the use of the stallion any time you want."

We talked on for a while then she took my hand, led me into the bedroom and we made love all night.

That morning she loaded her horses into her truck, threw her personal gear in, and after final hugs and kisses, off she went.

Mary and I stood there till the truck disappeared, then Mary took my hand and said, "Time for a cuppa."

Well, was I a gloomy grumpy bugger for a week or so, going about my work with a dark cloud over me, gardening, looking after Shaggy and the pups and also the sheep.

One night I was lying in bed enjoying my misery when the door opened and Mary said, "Can I come in?"

"Yes," I said.

Mary walked in, in a dressing gown, and sat on the bed.

"Stop being gloomy, John," she said. "I want more children and you're the only man I trust so what do you say?" and removed her dressing gown and slipped into bed with me.

I don't think I ever answered that.

Mary was 27 now and, funny, I had never noticed what a gorgeous body she had. It was a bit strange at first as we had been friends for so long and I had respected her desire not to have any men, but nature took over and a good night was had by all, as the saying goes.

Chapter Five

New life was breathed into the place, and once again I was planning the future. The sheep had been shorn again and with the money in the bank I had funds to do things. The accountant was advising me to spend money on the property to avoid losing too much on taxation, so I sat down to draw up a plan of action.

Mary and I fitted together like two peas in a pod. We talked, we planned, and began taking a great interest in each other's lives. Two heads are definitely better than one. Water is essential to all things so my initial planning centred on water preservation.

The land was contoured so that it was possible to build a large dam several acres below the house then I added smaller dams around the slopes just to hold up the water and slow it down. All these dams were connected by contour drains. Once this was all on paper I marked it out on the ground, then in came the dozer and it went to work.

Two weeks later, the slopes were scarred by fresh-turned earth and it all looked a bit horrible, but we looked past that to what it would be. We gave the dozer driver a good feed and told him how pleased we were with the whole job. While he had been digging the large dam he uncovered a small spring, so while we were on the veranda we watched the dam slowly filling.

The dozer man left, happy with his cheque, then Mary turned to me and said, "I'm pregnant."

I just didn't expect it after my experience with Gypsy. Just then the phone rang so I answered and it was Gypsy saying, "I haven't got much time, but put some good money on Wildfire," then she named the race and town.

The race was the next day so we went to town, found the local S.P bookie and put a 100 pounds on Wildfire at 20 to one.

We went to lunch at the best hotel to celebrate our son. Mary agreed it was a boy. Wildfire won, of course, and I collected my 2000 dollars and went and bought a Massey Ferguson tractor and a second-hand seeder. I had plans.

At irregular times, Gypsy would call and give us the tip but after the fourth time the bookie wouldn't take my bet anymore, but I had enough.

Ray wanted his shed back as his operation was expanding and Mary wanted to build a shed up near the road as a factory and a place to sell from. Thanks to Gypsy, we now had the money and the plan was put into action. A new steel shed arose with lots of windows and double doors facing the road with a gravelled parking area in front. It was great. It caught the breeze up there and the windows kept it cool. Moving-in day came, the Ute doing overtime to move the machines and all the leather and cloth. Mary settled into her new factory while her tummy slowly grew. She had two local girls doing the sewing, while she did the designing and made the original patterns.

Caroline was busy between the farm and the Toowoomba shop and when the girls had too much for their shops Caroline would take it to Brisbane and sell it to the large department stores. That, of course, led to more demand and a third sewing lady was employed. Country Creations continued to grow.

While all that was going on, unknown to us the bully next door tried to start a gossip campaign against us but the town wanted him out, not us, especially as Mary was employing people.

Whenever he said something nasty about us, the locals would counter with, "You watch them gypsies. They will slip a knife between your ribs," and other stuff like that. He started drinking heavily and it became a pub joke to touch him in the ribs with a dinner knife and watch him jump.

Now, I didn't drink except on rare occasions so I didn't know about all this until the land agent came out and said that the neighbours land was up for sale and the price was right as he had let the property run into disrepair.

Sitting down with the agent and a cuppa, I called Mary out and we got into serious figures. I could just buy the property and 1000 Merinos to put on it. I would have to do the forestry thing again but Mary was agreeable and it wouldn't be so bad this time as I could do a week on and a week off. Every second week the sheep would be on the new land and then on the forestry for a week.

The plan was put into action, papers signed, and sheep ordered.

Emily was still at school, she made friends fast and it wasn't long before girls were coming over to ride the horses. I believe the horses loved the attention now that Gypsy was gone. Some weekends she would ride off leading a horse for a neighbouring girl to ride. She would be back by dark all flushed and happy. She was 13 now and a very independent girl with a lot of quiet sense to her.

I guess that droving had taught us all a lot, making us all self-reliant.

I had a month to wait for the new land so I ordered seed, wheat, barley, oats, sorghum, as well as grass seed, and a heap of others. Then I climbed on my new tractor, pulled the seeder boxes, and started seeding straight into grass. When the neighbours saw this I had to take a bit of a ribbing about ploughing first before I planted my wheat. It was all good-natured stuff but I explained that I wasn't growing a grain crop but creating a diverse pasture.

I admitted that I was experimenting and would eventually settle on the seeds that did best. I also drove over to Killarney and collected kikuyu runners from the creek beds to plant in all the earth disturbed by the dozer. I enjoyed the whole process, and then, once again, the sheep arrived.

The sheep only had four months wool on them so I had eight months where I had to feed them on the forestry lease. It wasn't so bad this time as I could have them on the new 1000 acres if it rained and stay home, and each second week I did the same so I was able to stay in touch with what was happening around me.

The garden was lush and we were now eating off it. Mary's three hens she had bought so long ago had taken over the shearing shed and, as boys will, a rooster had come over from Ray's place and the next thing we knew we had chicks running around. It was necessary to build a proper chook pen so I got to work.

The building was easier than moving the hens and chickens but with the help of Shaggy's pups we caught them all.

Shaggy's pups were also due to leave home. The owner of the father got one free and we kept two females to cope with the growing flock, leaving seven for sale. We put an ad in the paper and told the stock and station agent. Now, everyone knew Shaggy due to the court case of the men who attacked us so the pups proved very popular. We gave one to Phil and Susan as they had acquired a flock of sheep. The others sold for a good price and everyone who bought them was happy as Shaggy had taught the pups well.

Now it was Mary's time to give birth. One night it was a quick rush to the hospital and by morning we had little Samuel. Mary stayed in hospital a couple of days. That was still possible back then, nowadays the ladies get sent home the next day.

The day I brought Mary home, I paid one of the sewing girls to clean the house and cook a great meal.

It was fun moving Samuel into his nursery, but like Shaggy, Mary had to do most of the looking after.

Then of course it was shearing time again. I brought in the 1000 sheep and the boys went to work. By the time the shearers were paid and the wool was sold, the cheques I got nearly replaced the money I had spent acquiring the new land.

Now I could help Mary for a bit. There wasn't much to do as Mary was a very efficient mum and all I had to do was sit on the veranda and nurse him occasionally.

This gave me time to think and it was time to sort out my Border Leicester's and start to form the nucleus of a very good flock of Border Leicester's. There was about 500 now so I brought them in to the yard and started sorting them out. I wanted a herd of ewes as I intended to sell fat lambs as well.

The older ewes were sent one way and the healthy younger ones another. In the end I had 300 good ewes. The rest I sold to the meat works. A trip in to see the stock and station agent to order another 200 Border Leicester ewes and some good rams. This meant I needed a ram paddock as it was no longer acceptable that I had lambs arriving at all times of the year and if I was to sell fat lambs I needed a uniform crop of lambs that I could sell all at once.

The pasture I had planted before the arrival of the second flock of Merinos was coming along well, a lot of the grain had come up as well as the lucerne and as it was all starting to seed I could see different grass heads appearing in the mix. Overall, I was happy with what I had achieved.

I remembered my experience in the forest of watching the grass regrow after the sheep had fed over it for a day. Now, how to replicate that with the herd feeding permanently on one area. The electric fence came into play again only I had to buy more. I divided the 2000 acres into 100-acre lots by putting stakes in, then I ran the electric fence around the first 100 acres. I put the sheep in there for a day then moved the top electric fence down to the bottom of the next hundred acres, then moved the sheep down.

The sheep soon got used to the system and I would only have to call the sheep and they would come, and Shaggy and the pups would bring up the rear. It all started to work as smoothly as I wanted. The grass would regenerate quickly after the sheep left and the mixture of grain, legumes and grasses gave me a much better pasture. The extra 200 ewes came as well as the rams who were kept separate till joining time. I was now getting on top of how I wanted to organise the property.

All this took a year in which Mary and Caroline expanded to four girls on the sewing machines, bigger orders were coming and little Samuel had his first birthday. Emily decided to mother little Samuel and she would take him off on a horse to her friends place. I crossed my fingers and let them grow up free of the do's and do not's that I had suffered. If Sam grew up as free and independent as Emily, it would be a good thing.

Each evening we would sit on the veranda chatting about the day's events. One evening as we chatted, Mary said quietly, "I'm pregnant."

"Did I hear that right? You're pregnant?" I asked.

"Yes," she said.

"Just as well," I said. "Because Emily has kidnapped Samuel."

"It's another boy," Mary said. "I just know."

The world was changing as well. The number and quality of cars increased so that traffic was getting thick at times. The contraceptive pill arrived changing life for all women who wished to use it, and there was talk of landing on the moon! Jet aircraft began flying overhead and we would run out to look and television arrived. We stood in front of shop windows, watching these flickering images and thinking that it wouldn't amount to much.

My days in the mountains seemed far away so I sat down to write to Beth and Alec.

Beth wrote back immediately saying how happy she was to hear that I was doing so well and that she was married again and they had taken back the farm and were working it again.

Alec I didn't hear from for a while and when I did it came from Moira. Alec and Mama were okay and still in their cottage, but she had married a whitefella and they had a small crop farm on the coast. Those pumpkin seeds we had planted must have had a powerful effect.

The S.P. bookie also became redundant as the government legalised betting and formed the T.A.B.

Gypsy rang one day to catch up so I told her she could start giving me tips again. Wildfire was getting too old to race but she had acquired other horses.

She rode them herself in the races, being one of the first female jockeys. From then on we would get occasional tips which mostly paid off. Gypsy was still single and it seemed she would remain that way for her whole life. Horses were her passion and no man could match it.

The property was running smoothly so I gave Mary the support she never got the first time as I had been spending all my time with the sheep. Emily was excited as well and on weekends she mostly took Samuel off on the horse.

Horses were making a comeback. Stockhorses, polo horses, pony clubs, draught horses were being trained for competitions so I decided to put my spare time into the horses. Emily, of course, had been riding them and brushing them occasionally, and of course horses kept doing what horses do so when I ran them in I was surprised at the number.

I had given Phil and Susan two young colts and Gypsy had taken two mares, now I had 13 horses. Four of the originals, three foals from the first drop, they were now three years old and another three foals from the original mare and two of the young mares appeared to be pregnant.

The originals I started giving a good brushing, the three-year-olds Emily had ridden them all, they just needed a bit of training and young foals needed a lot of handling. I went to work on them all. Gypsy had taught me everything to do with horses. One thing became apparent. I would need a new stallion and to sell the original one. That would be sad as he had given us such good service and we all loved the old fellow but we couldn't have him mating with his offspring.

Back to the stock and station agent and told him we needed to sell our gypsy stallion and buy a new one. There were no computers then so it took quite a few phone calls to track down a gypsy horse breeder. The gypsy horse breeder turned up one day, bringing a stallion he wanted to sell. It was multi-coloured and moved well and was overall a very nice horse.

He had a look at our fellow and got quite enthusiastic and wanted to know where we got him. I told him the story of the old gypsy and that I didn't know his name. He claimed that our stallion was one of the best of his type and he would do a swap for his stallion. I was happy, thinking I would have to pay quite a bit for the new horse.

We watched sadly as our old friend disappeared in the truck but that was offset by the antics of the new stallion, trying to impress the girls who looked on uninterested.

There was one more job I wanted to do on the property. I wanted to plant more trees. Mary and I discussed it on our evenings on the veranda and finally decided to buy deciduous trees as they would provide shade in summer, then lose their leaves in winter to let the sun in, also the leaves would fall and help to create a mulch. I ordered the trees and went to work planting. I kept the trees well spread as I didn't want to choke the grass out.

Chapter Six

The years passed with a shearing each year, a fat lamb sale each year, and the new horses being sold. The Gypsy Vanner horse society was formed as they were becoming popular as a quiet, versatile, reliable horse for children and less experienced people. Some of the older horses were retired and Shaggy passed on, but she left us with several offspring who were as good as Mum. Big Ears was old now but each night he would come and sleep near the house so we would give him a pat and spoil him with a couple of bananas. He still loved them.

Emily kept growing too and she had a great affinity with animals, so when she said she wanted to be a vet we found the money and sent her to veterinary school. She now runs around the district fixing animals and is doing quite well.

Mary and Caroline had built a large business with ten people sewing. It was getting quite hectic. During this time decimal currency arrived so we all became twice as rich as we were before as a dollar was ten shillings so there was two dollars to the pound.

One evening we were sitting on the veranda enjoying a cuppa when Mary said that her and Caroline had received a substantial offer for the business. Mary said she had been feeling like it was all too much lately and the offer included keeping Caroline on as manager.

We talked for a bit and it was Mary's business so she could sell if she wanted and the property was capable of supporting us.

I suggested she put the money she got with Michael in town as my original investment had reached a half million dollars now.

Our two sons, Samuel and Daniel, were now 10 and 8 years old, I was 30 and Mary 37.

Michael called me in and asked if he could use my money for real estate investments down the Gold Coast. He explained how the Gold Coast was taking off in a big way, high rise was becoming the normal and he explained about buying off plan and reselling again before the apartments were even built. I told him to go ahead.

Mary's business was sold and the new company moved the manufacturing into Warwick leaving us with a spare shed.

About a month later, we were spending our evening on the veranda when Mary said quietly, "John, I've got cancer."

It took a while to sink in. Then she carried on that she hadn't been feeling the best so she went to the doctor and found out that the cancer had spread through her body and there was nothing to be done. She had about three months to live by the doctor's reckoning. I promptly said, "Look, we have plenty of money. I can take you anywhere you want to go."

She held up her hand to stop me and said, "John, ever since you and Gypsy picked me up off the road, I have been happy, and this property has been my greatest joy, watching you turn it into paradise and me becoming a successful businessperson. It has been everything I ever wanted and you are the best husband I could have ever had. The boys are a delight and if I can watch them galloping around on their horses for a bit longer that's all I want, and your love to the end."

I hired a nurse to help and as Mary got weaker we put her out on the veranda so she could see the boys riding on their horses.

Then one morning, she was gone.

I went through the funeral in a daze. Phil and Susan came over, so did Ray and Caroline and what seemed like half the town. Mary had become very popular.

The day passed and Phil and Susan saw me home and stayed several days to be with me. Unknown to me they had sent word to the truckles to find Gypsy and tell her. The message got to her and five days after the funeral a big new horse float drove in and Gypsy flew up the stairs to hug and hold me.

Phil and Susan left then, knowing I was in good hands. I kept the nurse on for a couple of weeks to care for the boys, but I was in a mess. I dropped into depression and wouldn't come out. Sure, I rode around the sheep, explained to Gypsy what I had done and how I grazed the sheep. Gypsy rode with me and learnt the ropes but I was still very depressed.

I saw Gypsy down at the old gypsy wagon. She took the wheels to town, had new rubber tyres put on, greased all the bearings, checked the harness, then put the horses into harness and trained them to pull the wagon. She got it all going like clockwork and then one night she said, "I'm staying here, John. You are my family. I tried finding my real family but they refused to acknowledge me so you and the boys are my family now. Now you have to break out of this depression and you need to go and be stupid. You never had a normal teenage life; you were always so responsible. Now it's time for you to be stupid.

I want you to take the wagon and go to Nimbin and mix with the crazy people."

I put it off, had a deep talk with the boys and asked them if they would mind if I went for a holiday. I called Emily and had a talk with her and she promised to come out and be with the boys whenever she could. In the end I had to give in so I harnessed the horses to the van and off I went. Gypsy had thought of everything.

The water tank was full, the cupboards were stocked with food, and there was even a few cans of beer and a bottle of rum.

I hit the road and the first thing I noticed was the heavier traffic, but I was slow enough that they could pass me quickly.

It took a week to reach Woodenbong and I camped there for a bit to give the horses a rest. I was back in the green country with running streams which was great but there were also ticks and leeches and other biting creatures. Had I gotten soft? I had never really noticed all that when I was younger.

Another week down to Kyogle and another short camp there to rest the horses and then the final leg to Nimbin. I was only going there because Gypsy told me to. I thought I might stay the night and move on.

It would be a three-day trip as the roads were terrible. On the first day, I was leaving Kyogle when I noticed someone hitchhiking ahead of me. I finally caught up and then I noticed it was a girl. She asked, "Where are you going?"

"To Nimbin," I said. "But it'll be three days getting there."

"That sounds great," she said. "Can I come with you?"

She was quite pretty as all girls are so I said, "Hop on."

Annie was her name and she chatted about how wonderful it must be to live like this. We swapped stories and she got closer and closer to me until we were touching and there she stayed, cuddled up till I saw a lovely shady spot by a creek. I pulled up for lunch and to change horses. Annie immediately dashed off to the creek, dropped all her clothes and dived in. Well, Gypsy and I had spent a bit of time naked around our pool so I tied the horses and joined her in the water.

We played, dived, splashed around, and ended up making love in the water. I finally got to make a cuppa and lunch and we ended up dozing in the shade and swimming again.

The horses got a rest day as we ended up staying there for the night. We went for an early morning dip and then I remembered the horses and off we went. It took five days to get to Nimbin with the frequent stops but eventually the horses climbed the hill to the town and we pulled up in the main street. We drew instant attention. There were people in all kinds of crazy dress, the shop fronts were all painted with art, and people came up to pat the horses and wanting to look at the van.

Annie gave me a hug and said, "Thanks for the ride, I have to meet someone."

She was gone and I would have to get used to these casual relationships.

I had lunch at the cafe and asked where I could camp and was told to go down to the old butter factory. I set up camp there and began to settle down for the night but next thing I knew I had people gathering around the campfire, then the guitars came out, the music started and the funny cigarettes were being passed around. One girl had snuggled up beside me and passed me a joint which I dutifully dragged on.

I had been instructed by Gypsy to do something stupid, so I did.

I woke in the morning with another girl in my bed and memories of some wonderful sex. That weed certainly enhanced feelings. I made breakfast and fed us both and as there was nothing to do we went back to bed. Lunch time I checked on the horses. I had put them in a small allotment nearby and they would be right for a week. I fed them their usual tin of oats and they were happy.

The gypsy van and campfire became an impromptu gathering place at night and the music, dancing and singing went on while the joints travelled the circle. Most nights I would end up with a girl cuddled up to me.

One particular girl stayed a couple of nights and suggested we go out to the commune. I asked her if she could ride and she couldn't so I caught one horse and we double banked out to the commune, spent a day listening to some Buddhist monk talking, and we ended up coming home after dark. As we rode along, I decided to introduce her to some of the horseback love-making that Gypsy and I had invented. All I can say is it went down very well and when we reached the van all we wanted was sleep.

One day I went up to the cafe for lunch and as I walked along the street I heard, "John! John!" in an excited voice.

I spun around and was enveloped in a pair of black arms while I received a smashing kiss on the lips. It could only be Moira and sure enough, there she was: a mature woman, looking fantastic.

We went into the cafe to eat while we caught up on each other's history. She had two children which were with relatives and her husband had been killed in a car accident some time ago. She was down here visiting family.

We talked and talked over continuous coffee then wandered down to the van. Someone had started the fire and the nightly gathering was taking place so we joined in, puffed on a joint or two and by 10 p.m. we couldn't restrain ourselves anymore. We retired to the van for a night of love making.

In the morning Moira said, "I've been waiting for that since I was 12. Now I can die happy."

She wasn't about to die as she wanted more.

We rode out to see her extended family, she came in for a lot of good-natured teasing and I was accepted as one of them. It was these people who were to teach me about Earth Energies and the Rainbow Serpent.

Over the next six months I had my cards read, my aura photographed, listened to many speakers, declined a workshop that left people in the bush overnight to face their fears. I heard that California was going to fall into the sea, that a huge tidal wave would wipe out the Australian east coast, also all the prophecies about Earth changing and one saying that there would be no large animals left in Australia. That reminded me of a well-respected long-range weather forecaster, Inigo Jones, who had predicted a very severe drought that would empty the centre of Australia of all large animals.

During all this, I would go out to see Moira's aunt once a week to experience a bit of sanity. Moira had gone back to the farm to harvest carrots or something. Aunty sat me on the veranda and thanked me for lifting a shadow off Moira so she could now continue her farming.

Then started my lessons although I didn't realise it immediately. She talked about their culture and how the world was formed, about the rivers and mountains and the ebb and flow of energy and how we were one with the Earth. Each week she took me a little deeper into how they saw the world. She explained the consciousness field and how all our thoughts went out to it and in this field thoughts came together and then drew people together.

"That's why you met Moira," she said. "So that years later you could meet Aunty."

She explained that I was living on a property that contained a sacred site which in the physical world was governed by a large green crystal and I was the person to maintain the energy at that point to keep the Earth stable. When the Rainbow Serpent had black lines in it, it needed fixing. She taught me three songs which would fix these lines. I had to learn it in their language and as I could never remember poems at school I wrote them down as best I could. Aunty instructed me to sing them each day over and over as that would improve my memory.

I always enjoyed my days with Aunty.

Meanwhile back at the campfire the entertainment went on and then one night Annie turned up and we ended up spending the night together. Somehow our love making became very slow and gentle and we would feel as if we were floating in the clouds together. Next morning, Annie left early and I didn't see her for another month, when she came to the fire and once again stayed the night with the same result.

Life went on then one morning I woke up, walked outside, saw all these listless people with straggled hair and I had the thought I'd had when I first saw my horses. A bunch of hairy scrubs. It was time to leave. I had breakfast, caught up my horses and started to harness up. I was head down doing up straps when I heard a little voice say, "You're leaving, aren't you?"

I turned and there was Annie.

"Yes," I said.

"Where are you going?" She asked.

I replied, "I'm going west to be a drover."

She thought for a bit and said, "Can you give me a lift?"

"Well, I brought you here, I may as well take you away," I said.

It was early as we drove up through town but not early enough as Aunty was standing there.

"You're leaving, John," she said.

"Yes," I said.

"You must come home one more time, John and bring Annie."

I looked at Annie and asked, "Does she know you?"

"Yes, I've been seeing her regularly."

I looked at her and decided that the cloud had been hard at work.

Aunty climbed onto the seat and using her ample hips pushed Annie up against me saying, "He is your man now. Sit with him."

We drove up to Aunty's place and settled on the veranda. Aunty talked for a bit and said, "It's time for you to see the world of colour."

She lay me down on the boards and told me to do the relaxation she had taught me, then she came out with a burning stick, blew the flame out and waited till she had a red-hot coal on the end. She then lowered the heat towards my forehead till I could feel it getting hotter and hotter. It was reaching the point of unbearable when my body gave a jerk and the world of light opened to me, the vivid colours dancing all around me and everything I looked at.

Aunty left me for a bit then got me up and laid me to rest on a couch. She looked at Annie and said, "You will be living with him so do you want to see what he does?"

Annie laid down and went through the same process. Aunty left us then and went off to make a cuppa. Annie and I discussed what we were now seeing so we could accept it easier.

We spent the rest of the day talking to Aunty, getting her to explain the colours and what they meant, until we had accepted that this is how we would see the world from now on.

Harnessing up next day was a new experience, watching the play of colours around the horses. Eventually we were off on our trip westward. We drove along, becoming used to our new world of light and learning to interpret the colours we saw.

First we went to visit Moira's farm and there were all these vegetables laid out in neat rows. It was as pretty as a picture. We stayed there all day and a night. Lots of talking and wandering around the farm. Next day it was on up the valley to visit Alec and Mama.

They were happy we called and sat us down to damper and tea. I told Alec I was on holidays but didn't mentioned my property as I didn't want Annie to know yet. Next day, I hitched the four horses to the wagon and pulled the wagon up the steep climb to the Bunya Pine. Here I told Annie of my trip through the bush with Big Ears and how Alec had set me free to wander the roads. Off along the timber roads to Old Bill's camp. There was nothing left apart from a couple of rotting poles, then down to my first 40 acres. The house was gone, bulldozed into a heap but the property was clean with cattle grazing on it. Then down to Beth's place for a visit. Their farm was doing well and they had expanded by buying nearby properties.

We had lots of talk and we cracked up laughing when Beth described this ragged kid riding a mule without a bridle.

"I've still got Big Ears," I said. "But he's old now and sleeps near the house all day. I feed him bananas regularly. He still loves them."

As we drove away next day, Annie looked at me and said, "You have led an interesting life."

"Not so sure about interesting," I said. "Most of it was pretty scary and I just seemed to stumble from one thing to another."

Up the mountain then to Killarney where we camped for the last time. Next morning, I had Annie out of bed early, harnessed up, and put the horses into a trot. I hadn't told Annie about the property and I was in for a surprise myself for as we climbed the last hill I could see the old factory, and it was all different, painted bright colours with a big sign saying 'The Gypsy Wagon.'

As I pulled up in front I realised the factory had been turned into a restaurant. Written in smaller letters was 'The Trucker's Rest.'

I pulled the wagon to a stop and called out, "Can we get a feed here?"

Gypsy flew out the door and flung her arms around me.

"I thought you'd never come back," she said. "You were always so keen on droving."

"What's all this?" I asked.

"Well, the truckies looked after us so well," she said. "I decided to repay them. There are rooms at the back where they can sleep and have a shower. They all love it," she said. "Anyway, park the wagon over there and let the horses go, then come in for lunch."

She had slowed down enough that I got to introduce Annie to her, then she called out, "Michael, come here," and out walked Michael the financial manager.

"Good day, John," he said, and we shook hands.

"Michael and I are together now," Gypsy said. "So, he is part of the family now."

"Is he a stray?" I asked and got a smack over the head.

I set about parking and I let the horses go into the paddock. Annie was looking bewildered so I sat her on the seat and explained that we were home and that house over there was where we would live. I also explained that I owned 3000 acres and two boys who were probably at school.

She was having trouble taking it all in as she thought she had hooked up with a penniless drifter.

"Come on, let's see if Gypsy can cook up anything other than damper and stew."

Gypsy laid on a feed fit for a king and as the four of us sat eating Michael casually said, "John, you're a millionaire now."

My jaw dropped and I glanced at Annie and saw the same shock in her face. Michael went on to say he had invested in Gold Coast Real Estate and doubled our money, making me a millionaire.

"Gypsy," I said. "If you aren't married yet, I'll arrange it. We can't let him get out of the family."

Other customers started to pull up which broke our party up so we agreed to meet down the house later. I was walking Annie down to the house when she stopped and said, "I'm having trouble taking all this in. One minute I'm riding along in a gypsy wagon with a penniless hippie, and now I'm with a bloke who has land and sheep and horses and is also a millionaire."

"Well, I just found out about that myself," I said.

On reaching the house I showed her around and took her out to the garden and down to the creek where the sheep had gathered in the shade.

"This is truly all yours?" she asked.

"Yes," I said.

"Well, what do I do here?" she asked.

"That's a question we all had to face when we arrived," I said. "And we all found an answer and did very well as you can see. That restaurant was a factory originally, where Mary made clothes she sold, and she was doing very well for herself. So, you see, it's just a matter of finding what you want to do and then doing it."

The sun was getting low so I took Annie back to the house, sat her on the veranda and made a cup of tea for us. We sat there in silence letting Annie sort out all the information in her mind. Then the boys came home.

"You're back, Dad!" they shouted, tearing into the kitchen to get something to eat then racing off to catch horses.

"Stop!" I yelled. "Now come back here and meet Annie."

I did the formal introductions and then said, "Now go." And off they went.

We continued to sit, sipping tea, and finally Annie said, "I just want to be a mum, have a home, raise some kids and no arguments."

"You came to the right place then," I said. "Our golden rule is don't raise your voice in anger. You already have two kids if you can catch them. They're mostly caught at feed time though," I said.

Annie began to settle in, she didn't hurry but gradually took over the housekeeping, cooking and sweeping. Gypsy still lived on the farm and Michael came out in the evenings to help in the restaurant. Each Friday and Saturday Gypsy would sing while staff took over the work. She was very popular and filled the place with people on those nights. More and more truckles began stopping and even Bob turned up one night asking about Mary. He was very sad when he heard she had died. She was Bob's lost love.

The boys were everywhere. They were free spirits and looked after themselves mostly.

I settled back into the routine of the farm, moving sheep each day, watching the pastures to see which grasses and legumes were doing well. The trees were getting big and beginning to drop their annual harvest of leaves to enrich the soil.

Then came the news that Annie was pregnant and I decided it was time to think. Emily was well set up as a vet and had a partner now so she was okay. The two boys were growing like weeds and would need a future shortly and now there was another on the way. Samuel and Daniel were 12 and 10 years old now so I sat them down after lunch and asked them what they wanted to do when they got older.

Both burst out saying, "We are going to be drovers!"

"Well," I explained. "Droving really doesn't exist anymore. It's all done by trucks and the government now charges you for using the stock routes so perhaps you'd like a farm."

"Yes! Yes!" they chorused. "Just like this one." and off they dashed. I would have to see the land agent later.

I went and caught a couple of horses and suggested to Annie that we go for a ride and look at the serpent lines on our land. As Aunty had said there was a main energy point there, and we had best look for it.

Annie wasn't a good rider but the horses were so well handled by the boys who practiced the tricks Gypsy taught them that they were totally reliable.

The horses walked slowly while we scanned the colours, looking for an anomaly that would show us where the crystal was. Eventually we saw the spiral on top of a low hill. We rode up to it and sang the songs Aunty had taught us. It was incredible to watch the colours change and flow as we sang. We kept singing until the colour faded and became crystal clear. We then rode on watching the colours slowly improve as the new energy from the spiral flowed along the lines. We were coming to understand that the world was not just grass, soil, rocks and sheep but it was also an energy world of colour which supported the physical world.

We rode all morning mapping the colours of our land in our minds. Over time we were to learn that the energy world changed continually in response to human activity. For example, a quarry could create a negative line and negative human emotions could do the same, but in return a positive line could lift human emotions and improve life for all living entities. As we rode we sang our songs to lift the energy and found that our own energy lifted as well. It crossed my mind that if we taught Gypsy the songs and she could get the whole crowd singing them on a Friday and Saturday night, it could be very powerful, but I would have to talk to Aunty first to see if it was okay.

Riding back to the house our minds were fully occupied, absorbing the new information we had gathered. After letting the horses go we wandered up to the restaurant for a meal where Gypsy met us and introduced us to Larry, who was a tall dark fellow.

"Larry has asked if he can play music here," she said. "He has a band called Larry and the Mob."

"Are they here now? The Mob I mean," I asked.

"Yes," Larry said.

"Bring them in and let's hear what you play," I said.

Larry poked his head out the door and gestured towards a car and out tumbled five more members as dark as Larry. They had didgeridoos, click sticks, drums, and guitars.

Gypsy pointed to the band area and after a little shuffling around they began playing. My knowledge of musical style is very limited but after listening for a while my foot was tapping; my spirits were lifted and I discovered I was thoroughly enjoying the music.

"Well, Gypsy," I said. "It's up to you but they certainly lift my spirits."

Annie spoke up. "Mine too," she said.

Gypsy called Larry over and said, "You can do two hours Friday and Saturday nights, from seven to nine." And another lifelong friendship was born.

Larry then mentioned that Aunty had told him to come and see us. The cloud was working overtime, I thought.

While we were living our lives the world was changing as well. We started to hear about mobile phones, computers, climate change and carbon dioxide in the atmosphere. This raised terms like 'carbon credits' and gave rise to a lot of studies as to where carbon came from including methane from animals. Cattle got the most study while sheep were not mentioned. Also, humans were not mentioned and there is six billion of them.

Michael bought a computer first as his business came to rely on them totally. We bought one but I believed more in my brain than a computer, although Annie took to it and would feed me information. I guess I was an old stick in the mud, after all I still rode horses and didn't have a motorbike.

Annie gave birth to a little girl. Gypsy loved her and just took over except at feeding times. When the baby, Katie, reached one year old, the boys and Gypsy had her out on the horses. Sometimes we shut our eyes and prayed but we had all grown up on horses so it was sort of normal.

Annie felt like she had lost control of Katie so next thing I knew she was pregnant again and nine months later, we had Susan appear in our midst.

Annie hung onto Susan, she was her child and no one else was going to monopolise her.

Horses were once again popular. We now had 15 mares and the best Gypsy Vanner stallion that we could buy. I imported semen from overseas to add variety to the herd. The gypsy horses were very quiet and reliable so they became favourites for beginners and children, and also for pulling carts. I took them to the show each year and the boys and Gypsy would put on a show with them and that seemed to be enough to sell all the young stock that we wanted to sell.

The boys, Samuel and Daniel, were now riding in local rodeos and as Warwick was one of the biggest it was a good test for them. They won some events and then informed me they were going to follow the rodeo circuit. I let them go as boys must go and have a period of freedom before some girl would tame them.

This brought up their future again so I went to see the stock and station agent and told him I wanted two properties. It took a while but I eventually got two properties with good water and grass. I wasn't sure if the boys would still want properties in the area but if they didn't they could sell and use the money to start elsewhere. I leased the properties out and opened trust accounts in the boys names so the lease money could be paid to them to give them some working capital.

Little Susan as she became known was definitely Annie's shadow. She cried when taken near horses and was happy to play with her dolls and be a little mum. One of Shaggy's descendants had pups and Susan adopted one as if he were her own child. She brushed him, dressed him up in dresses and had ribbons in his hair. In return, the pup decided that he was in the world to guard Susan. We were happy about this knowing no harm would come to Susan while he was around. They grew up together like brother and sister and this started Susan on her career with dogs. I enjoyed Susan as well as she would sit on my knee and chatter away while putting ribbons in my hair or feathers in my hat. It was nice to have a quiet child for a change. Katie hung around Gypsy at the restaurant and learnt to play the piano, to cook, and serve, as well as riding every spare minute. She did pat me on the head occasionally as she dashed past.

The sheep continued to do well. Wool prices went up and down as did fat lamb prices, but rarely were both down at the same time so there was always a good income from the property. The pasture did well and I would reseed them every couple of years. The trees were getting large and dropping mulch each year. One year we had quite a severe drought and as I drove home through the failed grain crops and dead grass, I came upon my own pastures which still had a tinge of green in them and they looked good. I stopped the car and sat there congratulating myself as I had taken a lot of flak when I first started improving them.

We called Little Sue's pup 'Boxer' because he was a fighting dog and it was also a play on his appearance for rarely was he seen without a ribbon or two in his hair. Boxer grew much faster than Little Sue of course and soon he was carrying Little Sue around on his back.

We went up to the restaurant to eat fairly regularly, to talk with the truckles and enjoy Larry's music. Little Sue became the darling of the truckles as she would wander around chatting to them all and tying ribbons on their fingers. She had a thing about ribbons that girl.

One lunch time we went up for a meal and when we walked in I saw Big Red. We stopped and chatted and then Gypsy caught my eye and nodded towards a table and there I saw something I thought only existed in movies. There was a bloke dressed like a movie mafia boss with two big bruisers sitting either side of him. I walked over to Gypsy and she said, "That looks like trouble. Hopefully for someone else and not us."

Little Sue was chatting to the truckies with Boxer by her side. She went up to Mr Fancy Dress and started talking but he snarled at her and told her to bugger off and take her dog with her. Little Sue was obviously shocked and stood there, having never encountered this kind of behaviour before. Then Mr Mafia made the biggest mistake of his life. He reached out and pushed Little Sue over. Before Sue hit the floor, Boxer jumped and bit down hard on his arm and shook. We could hear the bones snapping across the room. He squealed like a stuck pig, yelling, "Kill the bastard, kill the bastard!"

The two bruisers stood up, pulling guns out but Big Red kicked his chair back, took two steps and hit one bruiser on the jaw, followed by the classic kick to the groin. That was him out of the fight, meanwhile the butt-end of a pool cue landed on the side of the other bruiser's head and down he went.

Boxer was still dragging Mr Mafia around the floor, shaking his arm and biting and chewing on it, and that's when he made his second mistake. He pulled a gun with his other hand and Boxer grabbed that arm and went to work breaking and chewing it to pieces. Then a pool cue smacked him behind the ear and he stopped squealing.

We were left with three Mafia bums on the floor, none of them in very good condition.

Gypsy rang the police and they arrived quick time. The boys gave them the story of how they assaulted Little Sue and of pulling guns to shoot Boxer and how they were stopped. The boys had gathered the guns and now handed them to the police. The three of them were duly carted off to prison and Mr Fancy Dress to hospital where the surgeons never could put his forearms back together so they remained bent and twisted for the rest of his life.

When one of the bruisers got out on bail and came to collect the car, he discovered that a truck had backed into it and the front was squashed. It got towed off to the wreckers and our local Holden dealer made another sale. They were all fined and released, never to be seen again.

It was free meals for everyone that day, after all I was a millionaire and they had all helped Little Sue and it didn't strain the budget.

The story went out on the truckie airways and after that Boxer was treated with great respect and no one ever acted aggressively toward Little Sue.

Back at the farm, Annie and I rode the property singing the lines when they looked dark. One day we were in town shopping when Annie asked me if I could see the darkness in people as well. When I paid attention, I discovered that I could so I said, "Yes, I can."

Then Annie said, "What if we sing the songs to the darkness in the people, do you think it might work on them?"

"We can only try," I said.

We would choose an individual and quietly sing the songs Aunty had taught us. Sometimes we would see the colours change but not always. We kept doing this each time we were in town, of course we never knew who the people were so we had no way of knowing whether it had an effect on their health.

It was six months before we heard our first story of how someone had got better from an illness that was supposed to be terminal. After that, we would hear stories of people getting well from conditions they'd had for a long time.

We couldn't say it was us as we didn't know any of the people but we took it as encouragement and kept singing when we saw shadows in people.

Warwick got a bit of a name as a healing place. Some gave the water the credit, some the pure air, some said it was spontaneous healing, the butcher claimed it was his good meat and the ice cream man said it was his secret ingredient.

Annie and I stayed quiet, as you can imagine the ridicule if we claimed we sang them to health, and besides, we wanted to be farmers not healers. We noticed that our property seemed to attract more storms. Some said we were on a storm track, others said that we were lucky, but once again we didn't mention singing the serpent lines as things like that just weren't understood.

Then the boys arrived home, both with young ladies on their arms, both serious about settling down. I got out the deeds to their land and took them out to their properties and told them if they didn't want that style of life they could sell them and do what they wanted. They also had money coming from Mary's will which was considerable so they were in a very good position to start life.

Katie was growing up as well and looked like she may take over the restaurant when Gypsy got tired of it.

Gypsy and I were now in our fifties and starting to slow down just a little bit. Annie was seven years younger and totally content with her home.

Annie and I noticed that some of the prophecies we had heard of at Nimbin were coming true. The big icebergs were breaking off the Antarctic and the ice on the North Pole was melting. As predicted by the scientists, the weather was becoming more erratic with wild storms and more droughts and floods.

The property carried on with shearing times coming and going, and fat lambs were a good price now. I could have expanded but I was content with what I had, it gave us time to sit on the veranda and drink a little rum which I had decided to like. Annie, me, Gypsy and Michael would sit in the squatters chairs, sharing a drink, and doing some reminiscing over early times. Michael told me I had three million dollars now. Real Estate was booming down the Gold Coast. He also had Gypsy's money invested and she was a millionaire as well but we were all content to sit on our veranda and watch the horses and sheep in the fields.

Little Sue must have inherited my desire for a home as well as Annie's wish to just be a housewife. As she grew she took over the housework and would top up our drinks as we sat talking. She also had a passion for dogs. I'm sure she could communicate with Boxer and she began training dogs, starting a group in town to teach people how to train their dogs. She also started training helper dogs that would help disabled people. She was always quietly spoken and often seemed to be in a dream world but she got things done and was quite efficient. She was an exceptional girl in her quiet way.

My 60th birthday came around. How did that happen? I realised getting older wasn't something one had to work at.

The ten-year drought was biting. The Darling River dried up and most dams were drying too. Brisbane and the Gold Coast were nearly out of water and they began building pipelines frantically and a desalination plant on the Gold Coast. No one ever dreamed that this would happen even though the scientists had predicted such happenings. My property was holding up well but I sold one third of my sheep so as not to overload the pastures. The large dam held up okay but our fishing hole in the river dried up.

In the afternoons as we sipped our drinks, we talked of our early droving days which really couldn't happen now as all the rivers and creeks we watered at were now dry and there was little rain to provide temporary pools of water.

In 2011, the drought ended in a devastating flood for Queensland. The Lockyer Valley got washed away, Brisbane went underwater, as did many other towns around Queensland. Our fishing hole was overfull which we didn't mind at all. A couple of our smaller dams were washed out and we had to repair them.

With the droughts and floods blind, Freddy could see there was going to be food shortages in the future. My early training came to the fore and I hired a young fella to work the garden for me and to do other work around. He was a keen young bloke so I put time in with him, teaching him how the property operated and why it was staying in fairly good condition. I thought he might make a good manager as I got older.

By the time the floods were over, I was in my early seventies and so was Gypsy. She still rode and sang occasionally but Katie had taken over the restaurant, so Gypsy and I discussed it and I decided to cut off ten acres around the restaurant and deed it to Katie.

I was selfish enough to want the property to carry on after my death so I sat down with Little Sue who was now big and asked her if she wanted to carry on, on the property after I died.

"Of course, Dad," she said. "I've always known that it was me who would look after the family."

"What do you mean by that?" I asked.

"Well," she said. "You will live a long life and most of the others will lose what they have and this place will carry on."

"Why will the others lose what they have?"

"Well, Dad, it's simple. Climate change will cripple them and a financial crash will finish them, but," she said. "I will keep singing for the rainbow lines and this place will survive."

"How do you know about the lines?" I asked.

"Because I can see them," she said. "And I hear the songs you and Mum sing as they travel the lines. I know all the songs," she said. "Even some you don't know. I hear them, you see."

I was dumbfounded. Here was the little girl we had raised and sometimes thought she might be a little simple and now we were discovering she was way out in front of us. I needed to let this sink in so we sat, sipping our rum.

Annie finally said, "That was a shock."

"Yes," I said.

We continued to sit and then Little Sue came back out and sat down.

"Dad, you know Bill, the young fellow you employed."

"Yes," I said. "Very well. He is a good bloke."

She said, "Well, Dad. He is the reincarnation of Old Bill that helped you and he is back to carry on what you began."

"How do you know that?" I asked.

"I can see his past, you know, and that young Bill was Old Bill.

I said, "Can he see the rainbow lines as well?"

"Yes, Dad," said Sue. "And I've taught him the songs as well. All this will be in good hands when you leave but that won't be for a long time yet." Then Little Sue said, "Dad and Mum, I've known for a long time that it's you two who are singing people back to health in town and with your permission I will carry on with that as well."

"Yes, do so," I said.

"I'll tell you all of it now, Dad. Bill and I are lovers and will remain so all our lives. So, you see, you can relax and be sure your land will be cared for."

All this had rocked me to the bottom so I said to Annie, "Let's go fishing."

We sat holding our fishing rods, discussing what had just been said to us.

"I feel redundant," I said.

"Me too," said Annie. "Why don't we buy the best air-conditioned car in town and go travelling north. It would be good to see coconut palms and the reef and when we come back, if the farm is still ticking along nicely, we will know that what Little Sue said is correct."

"Okay," I said. "But you heard her talk of a financial collapse so there is a bit I have to do first."

Next day we went to town and bought the best car we could and I went to see Michael. I told him of the conversation with Little Sue and asked him to buy one million dollars of gold and 500,000 of silver and to turn it over to Little Sue.

"If you want to protect your own money and Gypsy's, you had best have a yarn with Little Sue. She isn't the quiet little woman we all thought she was."

We drove home in style and told Sue what we were up to. Also, I suggested that when she got the gold and silver to bury it and pour a concrete slab over it.

"You could add an extension to the outdoor living area. I'm making you the manager and Bill the second manager. I'm sure you will work it out."

Next morning, we loaded a few clothes into the car and took off to visit Beth and Moira as well as Phil and Susan, then on north to the tropics. We took it easy, staying in motels and various resorts along the way. We went on boat trips to the reef, went fishing for big fish, laid under coconut palms, and swam in the lovely blue ocean. We didn't give a thought to home as we were suddenly totally confident in Little Sue.

We ended up in Cooktown, having travelled up the Cape Tribulation road. In Cooktown we hired a plane and flew up to Thursday Island, stayed the night and enjoyed a couple of rums overlooking the Torres Strait.

Next day back down the western side of the cape to Kurumba, where we stopped for lunch and gorged on freshly caught prawns, then across the base of the Cape to Cooktown. What a wonderful trip.

We had been on the road for six months so we turned south. Cairns was a bit big for us so after a look we went down to Mission Beach to swim and relax. We drove home in easy stages, getting to the restaurant nine months after we left. Kate was energised to see us and served up a great meal. Everybody had a mobile phone now, of course, and she rang Little Sue. Bill and Sue came up and a party was had by all. Gypsy and Michael turned up and Michael said that he had retired, so as we got merrier we decided to form an Old-timer's Club that would meet on the veranda each afternoon.

Now we are all nudging 80 years old and the financial world is anything but good, and the biggest drought in our history is biting hard and we watch the fires consuming Australia while the usual inept government staggers along.

I know Little Sue was right now, and no matter whether I live another one or 20 years I know Little Sue has it covered.

So, fill your glasses and, "Here's to Little Sue!"

THE END

Milton Keynes UK
Ingram Content Group UK Ltd.
UKHW052313101024
449474UK00006B/56

9 781398 428065